The

Tightarse

Tuesday

Book Club

Books by Duncan Smith

The Vortex Winder

The Maelstrom Ascendant

Cultown

Hammer and Heat

The Tightarse Tuesday Book Club

The Vast and the Spurious

Music Albums

Waves Upon Waves

Vortex Winder

The Maelstrom Ascendant

Cultown

The Tightarse Tuesday Book Club

Duncan Smith

Alfadex Books

Published by Alfadex Books, Sydney, 2020.

A CIP catalogue record for this book is available from the National Library of Australia.
ISBN: 978-0-9872228-7-9

1. Fiction 2. Humour 3. Social Criticism.

This book was first published as an e-book in 2018.

Alfadex Books orders and information - email: matthew.alfadex@gmail.com

Website - www.vortexwinder.com

Contents

Introduction

This book was meant to be ten short stories, but the first one grew so long it turned into a novella, which is a short novel. So, the book is a novella and nine short stories.

The long one, 'Marla Okadigbo,' may also be the most controversial and could cause a bit of a stir. At least, I hope so. The author, Sol Stein, once said, 'A long time ago I took an oath never to write anything inoffensive.' Whatever you think of that, it's certainly better to be bold than boring.

The stories vary widely in topic and tone. Some are serious. Others, like 'Hookup Hell,' are just for a laugh.

As for the title story, 'The Tightarse Tuesday Book Club,' let's hope that one is adopted by book clubs everywhere. They can have it for free!

Duncan Smith.

Marla Okadigbo

I - Winkler

The author, Winkler Jones, woke up one day to find his website had vanished. He rang his agent, Steve Cassel, who admitted he'd taken the site down but refused to say why - at least on the phone. If Jones wanted an explanation, he'd have to go to the office in person. It was with some annoyance, then, that Winkler found himself forced to take the train to New York.

Winkler fumed at home for a while, deciding not to go. Then he changed his mind and fumed for most of the train trip from New Jersey. Finally, he fumed a little more as he marched into the office of the Steve Cassel Literary Agency. He didn't bother to say hi.

'This had better be good, Cass. I'm on a deadline and you make me come into the city. We could have done this on the phone, couldn't we?'

'Sure, Wink. We *could* have, but whether we *should* have's another story.'

'What do you mean?'

'Oh, just a little rule I live by. Never say on the phone - or in email - what you wouldn't want printed in *The New York Times*.'

Winkler sat down, crossed his arms, and faced his agent over the desk.

'So, what's up?'

Cassel stared at him, his expression bland. Although both men were in their thirties, Cassel looked twenty years older. With his elegant attire, the bespectacled agent had the look of mature respectability. Winkler, however, would look boyish into his fifties. Both appearances were useful illusions. In private, Cassel dropped the mask and spoke like the hustler he was. Still, his relationship to Winkler was avuncular. Today, and not for the first time, he found himself in the guise of a prudent uncle scolding an errant nephew.

'How many times have I told you to watch your words?'

'Who did I offend this time?' said Jones. 'Was it something I said?'

'Something you wrote, actually - on your blog. That's why your website's 'down for maintenance' until we sort this out.'

'That bad, huh?'

Winkler did a quick mental scan of recent blog topics: PC Halloween costumes; the state of modern pop music; people who like things 'ironically.' They weren't that bad, surely.

'I give up,' he said. 'What was it?'

'Your books of the month.'

Winkler read a book every week, then at the end of the month, posted his thoughts in short, pithy reviews. Knowing how much work went into writing, he always tried to be complimentary. But the exercise would have little worth if he did not also venture some criticism.

'What did I say?'

Steve Cassel swivelled round to his computer screen and pulled up Jones' blog entry that he'd saved.

'Let me refresh your memory. I'll read it out loud.'

The Handmaid's Tale, by Margaret Atwood.

First published in 1985, this piece of oppression-porn is making a comeback. In *The Handmaid's Tale*, a societal breakdown has stripped women of all rights. In some unspecified near-future, women have been reduced to a childbearing role and are subject to full male control.

Thirty years after publication, you have to wonder why the book is so popular. But with Third Reich Feminism's campaign to persuade Western women they're more oppressed than ever, it may have been taken for a work of documentary.

Jokes aside, the book is really a work of naked misandry. It's based on the paranoid belief that men, given half a chance, are eager to put women into a state of slavery. Thus, collectively and individually, men want nothing less than complete control of women. This is shown in the pivotal scene at the point of societal collapse - shown in a flashback - where the handmaid's partner, Luke, is secretly pleased to gain power over her.

This may strike a chord with those who think oppression lurks behind every friendly face, and indeed, the new TV series version has found a ready audience. I haven't seen it, but caught the previews, which feature women in identical nun outfits - albeit in a sexy shade of red. It seems the Handmaid girls aren't oppressed enough to go 'full-burka,' but are still allowed to flaunt their faces. (Has anyone made the connection with Islam, or is that off limits?)

Atwood is a good writer - and I'm a fan of *The Blind Assassin* - but *The Handmaid's Tale* shows a preoccupation with the past. Why not imagine a better future full of empowered women? Oh wait, we already have the new *Star Trek*, the new *Star Wars*, the new *Dr Who*, and umpteen female superheros kicking the asses of men worldwide. Margaret, perhaps it's time to update your tale and give the handmaid some superpowers to lead a *Hunger Games* type revolt to a new matriarchal Utopia.

In the meantime, it's only a matter of time before an African-American author pens a dystopian tale in which slavery is restored. It's *gotta* be a hit. Right?

Steve Cassel swivelled back around to face his client.

'Well?' he said.

'Hmm - not bad. I think I got it about right. Don't you?'

'What were you thinking, Winkler? In three hundred words, you've probably managed to piss off the feminists, Muslims, and Black Lives Matter.' Cassel shook his head. 'And no doubt goddamn Margaret Atwood as well!'

Jones affected a look of innocence.

'What for? What did I say?'

'Cut the crap, Wink. You know very well what you said - and it's not on. Not if you want a career. You hear me?'

'Gee, Steve. Everyone's so sensitive these days.'

'There are some things you can't say anymore.'

'This is America.'

'Don't give me the this-is-America routine. You know you can't say anything to piss off the liberals these days.'

'Wait - *I'm* a liberal. Well, basically, anyhow.'

'Then what are you doing taking pot shots at feminists?'

'All I said was they're a bit paranoid if they think men are trying to turn them into handmaids.'

'You wrote Third Reich Feminism.'

'Did I? Must have been a typo. I meant Third Wave Feminism.'

'Sure you did, Wink. I guess that crack about the burka was a typo too.'

'Well - a bunch of women wearing identical nun outfits and

veils. What do you *expect* me to say?'

'I expect some common sense, that's all. Maybe you'd better lay off the book reviews for a while. Or at least run them by me first.'

'Like that, is it? I won't bother.'

Suddenly, Cassel thumped the desk.

'For fuck's sake, Wink, why can't you just do the Trump-bashing like everyone else! What's so hard about that?'

'I could, but what's the point? You know I hate clichés.'

'At least people would know your heart's in the right place.'

Jones looked unenthused.

'I can see the headlines now,' he said. 'Artist boldly goes where five thousand artists have gone before by slamming unpopular president.'

Cassel shot him a suspicious look.

'Don't tell me you support him?'

'Steady on, Cass, I don't support any of them. I'm an independent.'

'You've got to watch yourself these days. It's all about perceptions now - and if you screw up, you'll be all over Twitter for the wrong reasons. And if you've got any hopes of Hollywood ever adapting your work, forget it. You'll be blacklisted - and nothing personal, but if you're blacklisted our contract's not worth a pinch of poodle poop.'

Winkler raised his hands.

'Alright, alright. Wipe my review.'

'Good man,' said Cassel. 'I'll do that today, then put your site back up.'

Winkler yawned.

'Jesus Christ. We really could have done this over the phone. Can I go now?'

'Wait. There's something else.'

An odd look came over the face of Steve Cassel, literary

agent. A strange, furtive look. He left his desk, opened his office door to check for eavesdroppers. Then, satisfied, he returned to his seat.

'I gotta tell you, Wink, your review wasn't all bad. In fact, you've given me an idea.'

The literary agent glanced at his computer screen once again, then read the last paragraph aloud.

'In the meantime, it's only a matter of time before an African-American author pens a dystopian tale in which slavery is restored. It's *gotta* be a hit. Right?'

He turned back to Jones and looked him square in the eyes.

'So how about it?'

'I don't follow you, Steve.'

'The slavery book. When are you going to write it?'

Winkler Jones said nothing for a bit, then laughed.

'Get outta here.'

'Look, you said it yourself. It's only a matter of time before somebody writes a book like that. Why not you? Are you going to let someone else steal your idea? Publishing's all about timing, getting in ahead of the trend. Racism's a hot topic right now, thanks to Black Lives Matter protesting against white cops killing black teens.'

'You *are* serious! Looks like it's time for me to give *you* a reality check. I can't write a book like that cos I'm white. I'd get smashed.'

Cassel made a wafting motion with his right hand, as if batting away a fly.

'Of course it wouldn't go out under your name. We'd give you a pseudonym.'

'Really?'

'And a black persona.'

'A whole fake identity?' Winkler rubbed his chin. 'But what about publicity, interviews, book signings?'

'Who needs publicity when Black Lives Matter's making such a noise? Every time a white cop shoots a black teenager, they go crazy about racist oppression. They'll do all your press for you. All we have to do is wait for the next time some cop caps a black kid and away we go.'

'Wow, Cass. I've gotta say you're blowing my mind. You want me to write a dystopian science fiction tale where slavery's restored and the negro's back under the white man's thumb again. And you think the Black Lives Matter movement will be on board with that?'

'For Christ's sake, Wink, if *The Handmaid's Tale* works for feminism, I don't see why we can't come up with our own book to highlight America's oppression of the black man. But you've got to be quick, before someone else has the same idea. Why don't you bang out a book proposal and I'll shop it around? If we do it right, a decent advance isn't out of the question.'

'How much?'

'I don't know. Quarter-mill, maybe.'

'Really?'

'Then there's movie rights. I'm telling you, the sky's the limit.'

'Hmm. Maybe you're right. Tell you what, that sort of cash would get Sonia off my back. She's been busting my balls for a while.'

Cassel stiffened, as if Jones had said something deeply offensive.

'Let's get one thing absolutely clear,' he said, enunciating each word precisely. 'If this project goes ahead, it is a matter of complete secrecy. One word to Sonia, or anyone else, and you're a dead man.'

'Whoa there. I'm not a complete dunce. I don't exactly trust her myself these days. A bit of a payday, though, might smooth over the cracks in our relationship.'

Winkler Jones was silent for a while, focusing on the internal vision running through his mind. At last, he turned to face his agent and stuck out his jaw.

'There's one thing I want to get clear, Cass. If I do this, it's not about the money. I just want to do my bit to highlight the plight of the black man in America today.'

'And woman.'

'Yeah, and the black woman. I want to do my bit for the cause of race relations, to stand up for the black men and women of America in their continual struggle against the legacy of slavery. And I'll do that by imagining a world in which slavery is restored in 21st century America.'

'That's beautiful, Wink.'

'The implication being, of course, that slavery really *does* exist even today. The chains may be invisible, but they're there. They've just been internalised due to a racial hegemony which oppresses blacks systematically.'

'Love it. I guess you can pull in the academic crowd as well with that highbrow crap. Your book could become a mandatory set text. Hell - this is a home run for sure! Why don't you write up a proposal right now so I can start pitching it?'

'Can you give me a couple of days to brainstorm it? You know, just to be sure in myself I can pull it off?'

Cassel looked peeved.

'There's no time to mess about. It's only a matter of time before someone else does it first. But you know, if you don't think you can, maybe Cantor could do the job. After all, he's black.'

'Piss off! It was my idea.'

Jones suddenly shot his agent a look of suspicion.

'Hey, wait a minute,' he said. 'Why didn't you ask Cantor to write it anyway? He'd have a bit more credibility.'

The agent contrived a hurt expression.

'Professional ethics, pal. It was your idea.'

'Come on, Cass. I know you better than that.'

'Alright, you got me. I did think of sounding him out but I didn't think he'd go for it.'

Winkler Jones laughed.

'Pitching slavery to a black man. Tough sell, eh. But old Cantor's not seeing the big picture, is he? Well, I'll take the job. Only by making racial oppression explicit can I show the racism that's implicit right now.'

'You got it, Wink. See - no one can write this stuff better than you. Now get the hell outta my office before I call the cops!'

II - Sonia

On the train back to New Jersey, Winkler Jones decided to put his current project on hold. As soon as he arrived home, he brewed a strong pot of coffee and let his brain run amok. In an odd way, there was very little effort involved. It was as if the story already existed and was simply being transmitted to him. Well, that and the fact his plot just recycled a few standard themes from other dystopian fiction.

In any case, he was so absorbed in mapping out the story that night, he skipped dinner with Sonia, his live-in girlfriend. She made no objection and was glad of the time for herself. This set the trend for the next couple of weeks. Winkler was immersed in the work, and as a side effect, his relationship with Sonia improved. Not that it was really any better - there was just less focus on its worrying deficiencies.

Oh, it had started out alright. Don't they all? The fiery redhead had come on like a hurricane three years ago with a shared love of books, food, and laughter. In that heady first year, there'd been talk of marriage and even children. Yet Sonia had been slowly ground down by her job as a high school English teacher.

Sonia's teaching career had followed a similar trajectory to her relationship with Winkler. A rush of idealistic drive at the start; a long, slow decline in the face of disappointing reality; then thoughts of throwing in the towel - which about brought things up to date.

During their ever-more-frequent fights, Winkler accused her of being a workaholic, while Sonia dubbed him a layabout. That neither accusation was fair led to some heated arguments.

A typical fight had occurred the previous weekend. Winkler got up early on the Saturday for a walk, then brought back coffee and breakfast for them both. Despite his best efforts to rouse her, Sonia refused to budge, sending him out of the bedroom with some choice dockyard language. He decided to find it amusing that so angelic-looking a being could summon such filth. Glass half-full, right? Oh well - after her difficult week, she deserved to sleep in.

When Sonia did finally rouse, he suggested a trip into town.

'Sorry hon,' she said. 'I'm marking exams all day.'

She set up camp at the table in the living room, a stack of papers in front of her. Her long red hair, by now brushed into shape, flowed over her shoulders, setting off her creamy complexion and tastefully scattered freckles. Winkler, by contrast, was conventionally dark and handsome although shorter and more boyish than he would have liked.

'Tonight then,' Winkler said. 'Let's go for a couple of drinks and watch a movie.'

'Sure,' she said. 'I need a break.'

Satisfied, he left her alone to get on with it. But as 6pm turned into seven, then eight, she showed no signs of moving. Winkler became increasingly agitated, bustling round the house, sighing loudly, and slamming cupboard doors like a poltergeist made flesh. She ignored him all the while.

'I'll have to skip it, Wink,' said Sonia, at last. 'Or I'll never get through this pile.'

He sighed and sat down at the table across from her.

'If you'd told me three hours ago, I could have made other plans. Guess I'll go on my own.'

'That's not fair. Why do you get to go out when I can't?'

'So I should miss out because you're a workaholic?'

'You could at least show some solidarity. It's not like you have a job.'

He froze, knowing any reply would lead to a fight. He decided to be the bigger man and hold his tongue.

'Haven't got a job?' he said, two seconds later. 'I'm a writer. Remember?'

'I mean a real job,' said Sonia. 'Besides, you haven't put out a book since we met.'

'I'm halfway through revisions. Have you even *read* the chapters I gave you? When was it - *three weeks ago*.'

'I read all day for work, then at night prepping lessons. Pardon me if I'm not in the mood to read extra stuff as well.'

Winkler stood up abruptly and began pacing the room, as if fighting to control himself.

'That's lovely. No wonder you're under the strange impression I don't work, given my writing's invisible to you. Well, here's a scoop for you Miss English Teacher. You know those books you teach at school. Where'd you think they come from - the magic book fairy at Amazon? No, they come from real writers who work hard creating them. Besides - who cooked dinner every night this week and did all the housework? It's multiple choice: a) Martha Stewart, b) Mary Poppins, c) Caspar the friendly ghost, or d) Winkler as fucking usual? But no, I don't have a job.'

'Oh fuck off, Winkler. I get attitude every day from the kids at school. I certainly don't need it from you on my weekend.'

'Weekend? Is *that* what it is? I could have sworn it was a continuation of the never-ending Holy Crusade you call your job.'

'At least I'm making a difference in the world. Those kids need me and I'm not going to let them down.'

'Oh bravo. Nobel peace prize for Sonia. I guess you're really elevating the tone of drug transactions in the local hood. *Prithee, good homie. Avail me of thine finest crack cocaine, and compliments to thee and thine fair lady-ho.*'

'I don't need to listen to your racist jokes, Winkler. At least I'm helping some of those kids get out of poverty.'

'Sanctimonious when it suits you, I see. Which is odd, as you're normally the one bitching about them. I just have to listen to you whine. I guess that's another of my unpaid domestic duties.'

'With all the crap I go through each day, a girl's allowed to let off a little steam. Doesn't mean I mean it.'

'So I'm a racist, but you're just letting off steam. You know, Sonia, you've turned into a real pain in the ass since you took this job. The world won't fall apart just because you take a Saturday night off. Anyone would think you were Mother Teresa and Henry Higgins rolled into one.'

'Oh piss off, Winkler. Why don't you go out to a bar after all? I'm sick of the sight of you.'

'Don't worry I will. I need a drink just so I can stand living with you.'

'Sure. Be an alcoholic like your father.'

'Exaggeration as always. I only drink twice a week. But you know what? I'd rather be an alco than a workaholic like you.'

Sonia did not reply, but assumed a pious expression and went back to her work. Winkler folded his arms and looked rueful.

'By Christ, Sonia, we're the last of the true romantics, ain't we! What happened to us? And maybe it's the booze, but I can't remember the last time we had sex.'

He took a bottle of Scotch from a cupboard, and poured out a shot. He began to sing in a fine tenor voice, doing his best to butcher a jazz classic.

'A fine romance, with no blow jobs, killed by her day job, oh hell.'

Sonia looked up, a half smile on her face.

'Look. I told you, Winkler. The first two years of teaching are the hardest. That's what everyone says. Once I've proven myself, we'll get back to normal.'

Winkler upended the shot and poured himself another.

'So the warm, vivacious girl I fell in love with will return instead of this horrible changeling who's taken her place?'

Sonia raised her eyebrows, then with a sigh, turned back to her work.

III – Marla

That was a week ago, and Winkler didn't know how many more arguments they could stand. Indeed, such was the parlous state of their relationship that the new writing project was a welcome escape. No longer need he resent Sonia's endless hours working overtime. They gave him a chance to get on with his own book undisturbed. No more was he disappointed at her lack of interest in reading his work. It was a relief, given his agent's strict instructions to keep the project secret.

So it was that just two weeks after his meeting with Steve Cassel, he'd banged out six chapters of the new book. He headed back to New York to deliver the printed pages, then went to lunch while Cassel began to read.

Two hours later, he returned for the verdict. Winkler sat

in the desk, nervous as a schoolboy in the principal's office. Cassel's face was impassive. He sat there, suave as always, and ran a hand through greying hair he didn't bother to dye. He removed his glasses, then looked soberly from Winkler to the pile of printed sheets on his desk and back again. His face broke into a grin.

'Wink, you've nailed it!'

'You think?'

'It's a winner. Tell you what, I've been in this racket a while and this has got H-I-T all over it. Just hurry up and finish so we can get it out soon as the next cop pulls a gun on a black teen.'

'But what about the editing and book design? That'll take a year.'

'No way,' said Cassel. 'Not this time. Another year and racism might have gone off the boil. We're gonna rush this one through for once. I've already got you a deal.'

'What's the advance? Did you get the quarter-mill?'

'Nah, I couldn't swing it for a rookie. 50k, and even that was a hard sell.'

'Who are you calling a rookie? I've written four books in ten years.'

'You have, Wink, but Marla hasn't. You ain't writing it, remember?'

'Marla?'

Cassel handed Jones a sheet of A4 paper containing a small colour photograph and a printed biography. The photo showed an attractive young woman of African appearance, mid-twenties, with a look of warmth and spiritual depth. There was a name printed at the top of the page.

'Marla Okadigbo,' Jones pronounced slowly, getting his tongue round the unfamiliar words.

He looked up at his agent.

'I like it. There's a real ring to it. Where'd you get the pic?'

'Google Images.'

'That's a bit risky. What if they trace it? What if this girl sees her own picture on the back of the book?'

'Relax. She lived and died in the nineteenth century before slavery even ended. It's a black and white pic I had colourised and slightly changed. No one's going to know who it is. So your book will be 'written' by an actual slave. Pretty cool, huh?'

'Hmm. You know what? In a way, we're bringing that girl to life. Giving her a voice.'

'Absolutely, Wink. That girl's doing her bit for her people, even from beyond the grave.'

'Marla Okadigbo. I love that. That's not her real name, is it?'

'Course not. I came up with it myself.'

'Look, Cass, can you give me some of that advance?'

Cassel smiled.

'You'll get it when you deliver the finished manuscript. Not a day before.'

He picked up the printed six chapters from his desk and brandished them at his client.

'If you can come up with this in two weeks, you should be able to finish the job by end of the month.'

'Oh, come on, Cass, just give me 10k.'

'If you want to get paid, Marla, get to work.'

Once more, Winkler Jones paused to roll the name around his tongue.

'Marla Okadigbo.'

He raised his hands in surrender and made a sarcastic bow.

'OK, marzer. I obey.'

'Marzer?'

Both men laughed.

'Get outta here, Wink, before I call the cops.'

IV – The Watergirl's Pitcher

There was nothing for it but to finish the job. When he got home, Winkler Jones decided not to write any more that day. He would simply map out the rest of the plot, have a good night's sleep, then crack on in the morning.

That night he slept deeply and dreamt of green fields, savannah plains, and the young woman in the photo. She manifested as a subtle presence, infusing the landscape itself, then found individuation as a woman. Like a sunrise, her face changed from the flat image in the photograph to a vivid three dimensional reality. She came to him with a honeymoon smile and blessed him. He woke with an odd sense of yearning.

At breakfast the next morning, Sonia was prepping her lessons for school, arranging a pile of photocopied sheets in a folder. Her body language was cold, her replies curt. Without warning, she popped the question.

'Who's Marla?'

Winkler looked up from his laptop to find her blue eyes scrutinising his reaction.

'Say… what?' he managed, eventually.

'Are you cheating on me? Is this what you do when I'm away at work?'

'What are you talking about?'

'Who is she, Winkler? One of your impressionable young fans - is that it?'

'Where'd all this come from?'

'You were talking in your sleep. Don't lie to me. *Who's Marla?*'

'In my sleep? I do apologise, Sonia, for not having complete editorial control of my dream activities. I'll see to it my unconscious adheres to strict ethical standards from now on.'

'If you're having an affair, just say so.'

'Why would I have an affair when you sprinkle my life with fairy dust each day?'

Sonia picked up her briefcase and got up to leave. She paused at the door.

'You're an asshole, Winkler.'

'Love you,' he replied, as she slammed the door and left.

Winkler sighed, then went to his study to complete the synopsis for his book. It was a process he found useful - summarising the plot as if it were already an entry in Wikipedia. It helped him look at the story through objective eyes. Yet even as he sought that place of neutrality, he could not deny a surge of excitement as he surveyed the landscape of his new novel.

The Watergirl's Pitcher

By Marla Okadigbo

After the near collapse of Western civilisation in a nuclear war, America, in the year 2055, has fallen under the rule of a white, fascist government. African-Americans are now an underclass. Many live in grim urban ghettos that are little more than concentration camps, while the rest serve as slaves for wealthy and middle class whites. Some try to escape to Canadia, a rumoured multicultural paradise to the north, but most perish at the hands of the notorious Rompi, the white police force with a penchant for hair trigger 'justice.'

Kamali is a slave girl living on a plantation in Texas. Born in the urban ghettos of Los Angeles, after seeing her own brother slain by white cops, she was captured and sold to a Texan slave owner named Gillespie. Now she works as a lowly domestic servant, her main job fetching water from the river.

While carrying water one day, Kamali meets a young white woman who claims membership in 'Everest,' an anti-fascist resistance group involved in smuggling black slaves to Canadia. Kamali is too frightened to join her and defy her white masters. Yet later, back at the plantation, she is sexually harassed by Gillespie, who tries to grab her by the genitals. Kamali fights him off, but a seed of rebellion has been planted.

A few days later, as Kamali leaves to gather water, she is waylaid by Gillespie, who tries to rape her. Kamali fights back and strikes Gillespie with her water pitcher, killing him. Realising this entails certain death for herself, Kamali goes on the run. She embarks on a hazardous journey through fascist America, but is helped along the way by various marginalised minority groups, all of whom are oppressed by the white supremacist government.

After many dangers, Kamali at last tries to cross the US-Canadia border in a crowded bus. The bus is filled with minorities heading to the notorious Michigan death camps, where they are to be executed. Kamali intends to hijack the bus and drive it over the border to Canadia. Yet after a tip off, white cops board the bus, calling for Kamali to stand up and surrender. 'Who is Kamali?' the head cop demands.

At the back of the bus, a transgender stands up, saying 'I am Kamali.' Then a Latino woman does the same thing. Halfway down, a gay man stands, then a disabled woman pulls herself up out of her wheelchair. All are saying the same thing 'I am Kamali.' Finally, it spreads to the privileged section up the front of the bus, containing condemned white prisoners. They also stand, saying the same three words of solidarity.

At last, only one person remains seated - Kamali herself. In an ironic gesture recalling Rosa Parks one hundred years before, she refuses to stand. The white police chief grins, knowing he has found his mark. He fires his gun, yet the bullet only grazes Kamali's shoulder. He prepares to fire again, but the white bus driver strikes the police chief from behind, killing him. Everyone cheers, and the bus crosses the border to freedom. Kamali, bloodied but unbowed, raises her fist in a Black Power salute.

V - Voice of America

As soon as the manuscript was done, *The Watergirl's Pitcher* went to the presses. Then they waited - two weeks, a month, two months - until finally Winkler Jones got the call and found himself back in Steve Cassel's office holding a copy. The slender paperback - just 240 pages - had a real presence. The cover design was a winner. The red, green, and yellow leapt out and captured the eye. The back cover, featuring the colourised Marla pic, had been photo-shopped to perfection. Winkler could not take his eyes off it.

'Oh Cass, I think I'm in love.'

'In luck too. Did you hear the news?'

'What news?'

'Couple of young thugs got shot up in the Projects at Queens.'

'White cops on black teens?'

'Looks like it. This is our chance, Wink. One's dead, the other's in a coma. They're saying he might not pull through.'

'Alright!'

Winkler stood up and leapt skyward, both fists in the air. Halfway through the act, at the peak of his ascent, he performed a mid-air contortion, landed on his feet, and buried his face in his hands. After a second or two, he looked up.

'Fuck! That's terrible, Cass. What happened?'

'Routine traffic stop. One of the kids pulled a gun. Next thing you know, there's a shoot up and two hurt kids. They found drugs and weapons in the car. Dealers, I guess. Only eighteen years old, can you believe that? Their whole lives in front of them, taken away by police brutality and racism.'

'Were the cops white?'

'Let's hope so, pal. It's all over the news but they haven't shown their pictures yet.'

Cassel turned and refreshed his computer screen.

'Wait - there they are now. Oh no, what's this?'

Winkler rushed around to stand behind Cassel's desk and stare at the screen.

'Well, hello Nazis,' he said. 'That one on the left could be Hitler Youth.'

'Yeah, but the other one looks like a Spic. Fuck! That could ruin everything. The cops have really lowered their standards. Fucking affirmative action!'

'Come on, Cass, he's not that dark. What's his name? Larry Carter. That ain't no Spic name. Could be worse - Hernandez or something.'

'I guess so. I just don't want anything to ruin your big chance.'

'You're forgetting the victims. They're definitely black. Hell of a lot blacker than Carter, don't you think?'

'Winkler Jones, you're right. And here I am letting negative thoughts ruin our good news. Now that I look at him again, he's mulatto, or I'm the pope's uncle. Black mother, white father I'd say. Well I guess the apple don't fall far from the tree. Daddy's genes helped him pull that trigger alright. Goddamn racist.'

'So what now?'

'*The Watergirl's Pitcher's* going into every bookshop in New York by the end of the week. The new website's going live, along with those Amazon reviews I wrote up. Now get outta here, Wink. I've got phone calls to make.'

'To who?'

'The press, of course. This story's hot and one thing for sure, the tragedy of those kids' deaths won't be in vain. Not if I've got anything to do with it.'

And from there, it all happened so fast. Still, it wouldn't have happened at all without Cassel's foresight. As the old boy scout motto used to say, be prepared. They'd been ready to pounce and this was their moment. And lo and behold, just a few weeks later, Winkler Jones was back in the Steve Cassel Literary Agency, champagne corks a-popping.

'We've done it, Wink! Check out these reviews.'

Cassel handed a printed page to his star client, who took it with shaking hands.

'*The Watergirl's Pitcher* is a searing indictment of the racial condition of modern America,' he read. 'Literally a great metaphor for the American racial condition.'

Cassel seized the paper from Jones and continued reading.

'In a brilliant allegory, Okadigbo uses an explicit depiction of slavery to depict the implicit slavery of real-world African-Americans. It's an incisive analogy that hits home with its portrayal of institutionalised, systemic racism at a micro and macro level.'

'Wow,' said Winkler. 'I didn't know I was that smart.'

'Looks like you are,' Cassel replied. 'Listen to this: With masterfully spare prose that channels Hemingway or McCarthy, Okadigbo weaves motifs of slavery and privilege into a giant tapestry of oppression.'

Cassel beamed and Winkler punched his fist in the air. They high fived in triumph.

'So what now, Cass?'

'I've had a stack of media requests, but there's not a lot you can do in the publicity line.'

'Aw, what a shame,' said Jones in mock-disappointment.

'Just because you're off the hook, don't go on vacation yet. Or if you do, start planning the sequel. That's why I told you not to kill Kamali off at the end. I was right, wasn't I?'

'She should have died as a martyr. That would have been the most emotional ending.'

'So what's she gonna do in book two - lie in her grave?'

'That's why I made her pregnant at the end, on the bus trip. Her baby son was going to be posthumously birthed, then grow up to lead the people to revolution.'

'That's sexist, pal. You can't have a man succeeding where Kamali failed. Maybe if you made it her daughter... '

'Or granddaughter. Kill the son at the end of book two, then *his* daughter grows up to lead the Black Power revolution in book three.'

This idea shut Cassel up for a moment. He stroked his chin thoughtfully.

'Her granddaughter?' he mused. Then he waved it away. 'Nah, it's getting too complicated. Kamali's all you need. If it ain't broke, don't fix it.'

'OK - but where do we go for the sequel?'

'You're the creative genius, Wink. You tell me. But you know what I loved in *Watergirl*? All the little sci-fi touches. That scene at Mount Rushmore where Kamali saw the new lot of carved president faces - Reagan, Bush, and Trump, but Obama's had fallen off. That killed me! Always did love that stuff, even as a kid.'

'You don't think it was too much a *Planet of the Apes* rip off?'

'A rip off? You kidding me? A tribute more like. If you can get more of that stuff in book two, it'll kick ass. Go for your life, kid.'

'Righto, Cass.'

'By the way, Sunday week. You've got a feature in the *New York Times Magazine*. You wouldn't believe how much of my ass they were trying to kiss just to get a hold of Marla.'

'That must have been awkward. Are you sure they won't find out?'

'Long as you don't say anything, Wink, how can they? Meanwhile, Marla's absence works in our favour. It's all about mystique. An underrated marketing tool these days, but we're gonna use it like you wouldn't believe.'

Steve Cassel grinned, extended a hand, and uttered what was, by now, their goodbye catchphrase.

'OK, Wink, that's enough. Now get outta my office before I call the cops!'

The Sunday of the following week, Jones was up at 6am to read *The New York Times Magazine* article.

Marla Okadigbo: Rising Voice of Black America

She peers out from a publicity still. The most reclusive American author since J.D. Salinger, shy genius Marla Okadigbo rarely leaves her New Orleans home. The exact location remains unknown, which only fuels speculation on her whereabouts. Some say she's returned to Africa, others that she's living alone in LA, while wilder rumours place her in the New York Projects preparing to lead a revolution against white America. No one knows for sure. Indeed, Okadigbo is harder to find than Kamali, heroine of her breakthrough novel, *The Watergirl's Pitcher*.

When pressed, literary agent Steve Cassel simply shrugs. 'Marla is Marla. It's not for me to privilege my white perspective by telling her what to do. She'll talk when she's ready.'

Cassel has reportedly fielded offers of more than half a million dollars for an Okadigbo speaking tour, but his enigmatic client is unmoved. 'Sorry folks, no dice,' says Cassel. 'Marla wants to invert traditional media power discourses, not enable them. Translation - she hates the press. Nothing personal, guys!'

With the reclusive genius unwilling to speak for herself, it's left to others to sing her praises. Lucy Idaho, professor of Literature and Gender Studies at UC Berkeley calls her the most important writer of our generation. 'Marla is something else,' gushes Idaho. 'She's the master of spare, unembellished prose. When Hemingway did it, it was boorish machismo. When Marla does it, she's using masculine idioms to undermine white, male racism in a way that's truly exhilarating. It's an authentic interrogation of a cultural hegemony that's long overdue.'

For less academic fans, *The Watergirl's Pitcher* is a trainspotter's delight for its pastiche of references to science fiction classics: from *Star Wars* to *1984* to feminist dystopia *The Handmaid's Tale*. This, however, has raised a few eyebrows. One anonymous critic called it 'derivative,' and even 'plagiaristic.' Yet Professor T.J. Woodman of Indiana University laughs off the charge. 'It is literally impossible for the black man to steal from the white man. You could pay reparations for a hundred years and the debt from slavery would only have *begun* to be paid.'

As Lucy Idaho explains, 'Marla's use of science fiction tropes is an ironic appropriation of motifs favoured in white cultural discourses. Not to mention all the clever little literary touches. I mean, the slave owner, Gillespie who tries to rape Kamali. It's an obvious reference to the great African-American musician, Dizzy Gillespie. And what was his instrument? The trumpet. A cheeky allusion to Donald Trump, while simultaneously paying tribute to a black cultural icon.

At that point, Winkler stopped reading and laughed out loud. Gillespie... Trump? He hadn't thought of that, but he'd take it - and get some more of that sort of stuff in book two as well. He decided to treat himself and Sonia to a slap up cafe breakfast. When he tried to wake her, however, she refused to budge and eventually told him to stop harassing her. He shrugged, smiled, and went off to enjoy his breakfast alone.

VI - The Haunting

Winkler Jones sat in his writing room, a 'blank canvas' before him. Where to go for book two? More of the same, or something new? It was the usual sequel conundrum. And should he wrap up the story in book two, or hold out for a trilogy? He knew what Cassel's answer to that would be.

Of course, given that Kamali had escaped to the multicultural paradise of Canadia, there was no real need for a sequel. After all, now she was no longer oppressed, any story set in Canadia would be deadly dull and a sales disaster. No, he had to contrive some reason for her return to the United States. *I struggle therefore I am.* That's how it was and would always be. Or why bother?

His creative process this time was a more conscious version of what he'd done for *Watergirl*, which was the jackdaw's task of lifting a number of ideas from past dystopian books and films, and weaving them into his own story. Yet now the audience was real rather than hypothetical, he felt self conscious and a little wary. 'Marla' had been given a free pass due to the nobility of her cause, but perhaps this time he should do it with a tad more subtlety. This was the condition he kept in mind as he set about studying as many fictional dystopias as possible.

Unfortunately, the new research project did little for the state of his relationship.

'Why do we have to watch all this science fiction crap?' Sonia complained one Saturday night.

'*Logan's Run* isn't just science fiction,' Winkler replied. 'It's about how to handle the social problem of aging in a society with limited space and resources. People live in a domed city and have hedonistic lives until they turn thirty. Then they're killed in a public ceremony called Renewal.'

'Too heavy. I'm not in the mood.'

'Or we could watch the *Planet of the Apes* remake. It's really about racism and the fight for social justice.'

Sonia rolled her eyes, a habit that was beginning to grate.

'I've just marked a hundred and twenty exam essays, in barely legible handwriting, on the fight for social justice. Can we watch something else?'

'Don't you care about racism?'

'Of course. I'm just getting sick of hearing about it.'

'You'd be even more sick of it if you were the victim.'

'Gimme a break. If you're going to start on white privilege or something, I'm off to bed.'

'Aren't these issues important?'

'Don't lecture me, Winkler. I do my bit for social justice

every day at work just by showing up. Not that most of those young hoodlums could care less but, you know... I show up. So I don't need this political crap rammed down my throat at home too.'

'We don't have to watch a movie. Want to go out?'

'I'm too tired.'

'Gee, Sonia, you're a real life of the party.'

'You know what? Screw this. I'm going to bed.'

'I'll just grab a six pack and watch *Logan's Run* on my own, will I?'

'Knock yourself out.'

'Hey Sonia. It's your thirtieth in July. Just think - if you were in *Logan's Run*, you'd only have three months to live.'

'Sounds good to me.'

'Yeah - that would solve a few problems, wouldn't it?'

Sonia gave him the finger and went to bed. In a way, Winkler was relieved as it allowed him to return to his obsession with the *Watergirl* sequel. He went over the problems again, one by one: plot, character, themes, the plagiarism issue, and so on. Yet, there was the 'other problem' too. The one he still barely acknowledged even to himself. That problem was Marla Okadigbo herself - or rather, the young woman in the photograph.

He'd kept on returning to the picture. At first, he'd studied it purely for immersion in the role. Yet after dreaming about her on two successive nights, he began fixating on the image to a degree that surprised him. Who was this woman? He found himself making internet searches for 'slave girls' or 'nineteenth century black women' in the hope of tracking her down. When this failed, he resorted to phoning his agent.

'Hey Cass, can you send me that photo of Marla in digital? Where'd you find it?'

There was a silence, then a cold reply.

'Who is this?'

'Come on. It's me, Wink.'

'This office is not currently accepting new clients. For any urgent business, call my secretary to make a personal appointment.'

The line went dead. Looked like Cassel was serious about the need for secrecy. Alright then, he'd take another day searching for Marla online, and head back to New York if she didn't show up.

He began at once, but there was no quick resolution. Indeed, as he went down the rabbit hole of Google search results, he somehow found himself studying the history of American slavery. It was a topic he'd never before deemed of much interest. Now he could think of little else. As he studied, he began identifying with Marla's perspective.

The next afternoon he found her. As he scanned the umpteenth obscure photo archive, the image jumped out at him. Even allowing for Cassel's image manipulation, it was certainly her. With a triumphant cry, he immediately began checking the surrounding images in the hope of locating a second, or even a third, photo of the same girl. Yet that solitary first image was the only one to emerge.

He saved the picture to his computer, then blew it up as large as it would go. The resolution was surprisingly good for a vintage black and white shot, and when the girl's face first appeared at larger size, he felt an emotional surge.

Then there was the more disturbing aspect, the one he tried to ignore. He began to feel Marla was somehow 'around.' As he went about his day, the familiar sights and conditions of twenty-first century life seemed to have attained a fresh quality, as if he were seeing them anew. Several times, for example, domestic tasks seemed elevated beyond the mundane. There was a sense of wonder after using the microwave, or running the dishwasher. A new self consciousness was at play. The closest analogy he could recall was being stoned on dope or LSD, when the familiar had become strange. Now, as then, he felt 'wondering eyes' looking out, at home, and even more so when he ventured into the town.

This sense was not ever-present. It came and went like a breeze, and its whimsical nature made him moody. He found himself fluctuating between a rather manic excitement, dreamy yearning, or listlessness and irritation. One day he realised, with some surprise, that he was in a state of youthful infatuation, such as he'd not felt for several years. And all the while, he kept returning to the picture of Marla.

For a time, he made an effort to snap out of it, even dropping the entire project for three days as he went upstate to clear his head. Yet even there, despite his denials, he felt a foreign consciousness teasing round the edges of his identity.

At a loss over how to overcome the strange affliction, he turned to his creative outlet and threw himself once more into the world of *The Watergirl's Pitcher*. He returned home to continue work on the new book.

VII – The Review

As he grappled with the *Watergirl* sequel and strange obsession with Marla, Winkler consoled himself that at least his writing career was a hit. *The Watergirl's Pitcher* was a smash, and with whispers of a movie deal, his money woes were probably over as well. Yet he was bothered by the growing dissonance between his personal and professional life. He was now a bestselling author, yet relations with Sonia, while not overtly hostile, remained cold and apathetic.

Both used their work as a distraction from their failing relationship, and each resented the other. Winkler was peeved by Sonia's workaholism and ongoing sense of martyrdom. Sonia, in turn, continued to see him as a layabout author with few prospects. Sensing her attitude, Winkler felt a rising sense of grievance at an assessment so wide of the mark. In such a mood, he went close to revealing the truth about *The Watergirl's Pitcher*. Of course, Cassel had advised - nay, threatened - him so adamantly that he held his tongue.

He settled instead on the tactic of leaving a copy of the book in prominent places around the apartment - the bedside table, the kitchen bench - or conspicuously reading it while she was around. Yet Sonia, concerned only with her ever increasing workload, failed to take the bait. Here was an English teacher with no desire to read outside her professional obligations. This annoyed Winkler to the extent that his efforts finally lost any subtlety at all.

'Have you read this?' he said at last, thrusting the book in front of her like a pushy bible salesman.

She brushed his hand away, without looking up.

'What is it? I'm busy.'

'It's the book everyone's talking about. You really should read it.'

'Who's got time? Uh, I guess people without a job.'

The cheap shot hit home.

'Well, that's lovely. Nought to a hundred on the bitch-o-meter. What the hell's wrong with you?'

Sonia prepared an angry rebuke, then caught herself and sighed.

'I'm sorry. That was uncalled for. I haven't been myself lately.'

'You and me both, honey.'

He reached out a tentative hand and touched her shoulder.

'Show me,' she said. He held the book up for inspection.

'You can borrow it, if you like. Not a bad read.'

She turned back to her laptop, and preparing the day's

lessons.

'Maybe in the holidays.'

'I'll leave it on the table. OK?'

She grunted and went back to her work. Yet to Winkler's surprise, later that night in bed, Sonia picked up *The Watergirl's Pitcher* and read a few pages, before falling asleep. As he turned off the lamp, a small smile of satisfaction came to his lips.

He was pleased to see her reading continue over the last three weeks of the school term. Indeed, every morning, he obsessively noted the location of her bookmark to see how far through she was. He refrained from asking her opinion of the book, not wanting to break the spell. He realised now how much he craved her approval, and her respect. In their early days it had been intoxicating to hear her rave about his writing. Over time, her ardour had cooled. Secretly, he hoped *Watergirl* would return them to the honeymoon period they'd once known.

At last, just as the school term came to an end, Sonia finished the book. That night, Winkler was determined to get her opinion. And when her glowing review came in, he would - Cassel be damned - reveal his authorship of the work. Then, in a grand Romantic gesture, he'd tell Sonia that if the movie deal came through, they'd have enough money for her to quit teaching and do something else with her life.

He had patience enough to cook her a special dinner and ply her with wine. Then, half an hour after dinner, with them both a bit drunk, he could wait no longer.

'By the way,' he said. '*The Watergirl's Pitcher*: what did you think?'

'It was OK, I guess,' Sonia said, after a pause.

Winkler waited to see if any more drips were going to come from the seized-up old tap. They didn't.

'And?' he pressed.

She looked at him warily.

'What do you want – a written review?'

'I just want to hear your thoughts. After all, you're an English teacher. I'm interested in your thoughts on this popular work of American literature. Is that so outrageous?'

'Why's it such a big deal to you? You're acting weird.'

'You know, Sonia, when we met we used to talk about books a lot.'

'We used to do a lot of things.'

'Tell me about it. No – don't. Just tell me about this book. For old times' sake.'

Sonia stared out the window for a while.

'Want to know something strange?' she said at last. 'It sort of reminded me of your stuff.'

'Is that so?' said Winkler, a smug smile starting to form.

'Just odd lines here and there, the writing style. But an inferior version. A sort of bad copy, if you know what I mean.'

'Oh really?' he said, the smile stillborn.

'Yeah. All the media hype about this book, I really expected better. They're talking like this Marla chick's the greatest author since Harper Lee. Sorry, I don't see it. You know what? You're three times as good a writer. Wish you had half her success, right?'

With a rueful smile, she reached out and touched his cheek.

'You don't think it's a good book?' he said, struggling to process her reaction.

'Not really, but I'll probably have to teach this crap at school in a year or two anyway. That's why I read it.'

Winkler was lost for words. Then, floundering for a resolution, pressed her further.

'What's so bad about it? Everyone else seems to love it.'

Sonia sighed, as if struggling through a poor student essay.

'The whole premise is stupid, for a start. As if slavery's going to make a comeback.'

'It might.'

'Oh bullshit. It's just paranoia and a persecution complex. But are any of the critics going to say that? No, they're taking it all so seriously like it could really happen.'

Sonia laughed cruelly.

'And some of those corny scenes!' she said. 'I mean, that Mt Rushmore bit. When did they make the new presidents' faces? Bush, Obama, and the rest.'

'2035, I believe,' said Winkler stiffly.

'Yeah, like that's going to happen. And the part where Kamali was smuggled to Canada by all the minority groups. The Latinos, the LGBTs and the rest. Gimme a break!'

'Well - they were all oppressed by the white supremacist regime! Why wouldn't they help each other?'

'Right. So that's why they all stood up on the bus at the end when Rosa - sorry, Kamali - refused to stand and they're all chanting "I am Kamali." Sheesh.'

'You didn't find it moving?'

'Seriously, Winkler, I nearly laughed out loud. How is this Okadigbo woman allowed to rip off *Spartacus* anyhow? At school, we call that plagiarism.'

'When you do it deliberately and make it clear, it's not theft it's appropriation. It's a postmodern thing. Maybe you haven't heard of it. When you're dealing with a serious topic like black slavery, I think it's justified, don't you?'

Sonia gave him a scornful look.

'Just a heads up for you, Winkler. Spartacus was white. Blacks aren't the only ones who've been enslaved.'

'Gee, thanks for enlightening me, Teach. Guess who enslaved him? The white Roman empire.'

'There were slaves in Africa too. Owned by blacks. Did you know that? And let's not forget Islamic slavery either.'

'Don't take that patronising tone with me, Sonia. You know what? You're coming over like some kind of racist. Is this the sort of person we've got teaching in American schools now?'

'Fuck you, Winkler! You've been a real jerk lately. Since when have you been the big race campaigner?'

'Well *excuse me* for caring about issues that affect my own country. How terrible. I guess I should just stick a big cigar in my mouth and get on with my white privileged life.'

'You don't have to work. That's certainly one privilege you enjoy.'

Winkler stood up and shoved his chair so hard it overturned.

'Don't have to work? I'm a writer and I've been working my ass off for the last few months. Not that you'd notice, you're so self absorbed. God, you're pathetic. You're an English teacher - you're supposed to respect writers. Except the one you actually live with, of course, who you treat like he's some kind of panhandler bumming smokes in the subway. Well, guess what? I work on my writing every day. Why not try it yourself and see how easy it is?'

'Yeah right, Winkler. When you have to teach English and History to a bunch of teenage thugs, deal with a staffroom full of bitches, and mark eight hundred papers in your spare time, then get back to me about how hard you work.'

'Staffroom full of bitches, eh? I guess you fit right in. They probably all take notes watching you just to pick up tips.'

Sonia stood up, and tried to shove him, but he caught her arms and pushed them away.

'You want to talk about slavery?' she said. 'If anyone's a slave, it's me. Meanwhile I don't know what most of the school's ex-students are doing. Hustling, scoring drugs, and shooting people, half of them. One thing they're definitely not doing is working.'

'That's just a lot of racist stereotypes. Most of those poor kids can't even get jobs because of white racism.'

'What a lot of crap. You want a history lesson? When did slavery end in the United States? 1865. That's over a hundred and fifty years ago! Don't you think it might be time to - I don't know - *get over it?*'

'What about segregation?'

'Legal segregation ended in 1954, and the Civil Rights act was 1964, but blacks are still obsessing over oppression.'

'Well, they *are* oppressed. They've got worse education, worse jobs. They get locked up in jail, shot. That's white America does that. White. Fucking. America!'

'Oh yeah? How do you know? Cos I'll tell you what *I* know. Our school does *everything* to help them. We *go out of our way*. And some of them are good kids. They work hard, and you know what? They can achieve anything they want to. But the rest of them? Some of the scumbags actually try and stop the good kids from working, like it's an affront to their values or something. Acting white, they call it. Like it's a sell out to try and be a good citizen and make something of yourself. The rotten apples want to spread their rot to everyone else.'

'Well, I think it's great you're trying to make a difference.'

'We go out of our way to help them - fat thanks we get. And you've got the nerve to call me a racist!'

'I didn't mean you personally. It's the system that oppresses blacks.'

'Does it, Winkler? Does it? What's this mysterious system that makes people do things against their will? Where is it? All I can talk about is the individual. If I was really allowed to speak my mind, you know what I'd tell the kids at school? I'd say, hey kids, here's my number one tip. If you don't want to be oppressed by the system, here's what to do - get an education. Study hard, get good grades. Don't take drugs, don't do crime. Don't get pregnant at fifteen. Don't hang out with thug losers.

Work hard, get a good job, and see what happens.'

'Wow. So easy. Yeah I guess that's it!'

'And here's my second tip. Shut up about oppression and racism. Just GET OVER IT.'

'Yeah, just like that. *Get over it*. Why didn't I think of that before? I must email the president.'

'And as for this self-pitying, paranoid, lying piece of crap - you want to know what I think of it, Winkler? Do ya wanna? Alright, then, here's my review.'

Sonia picked up the paperback of *The Watergirl's Pitcher* and ran to the window of their third floor apartment.

'Sonia. What are you doing?'

'You want my review, Winkler? Here it is. Wheeeeee!'

And with that cry of rage, Sonia flung *The Watergirl's Pitcher* out the window and far off into the night, where it made a graceful arc through the sky and crashed onto the pavement on the other side of the street. Winkler rushed to the window to locate its resting place.

'You lunatic! You could have hit a car and killed someone.'

'I know. It was just my daily effort to oppress someone. I try to oppress at least one person every day. Dang, looks like I missed. I'll have to try harder tomorrow, if I can find time in my busy schedule of trying to educate and inspire America's youth.'

Then, without warning, Sonia collapsed onto the couch and began crying - loudly, and with no attempt to stop.

Winkler, truly shocked by the turn of events, sat beside her awkwardly, wanting to take her in his arms, but uncertain how the gesture would be received. He also knew their relationship was almost certainly over.

'What happened to us, Sonia?' he said eventually.

She continued to cry. At last, he summoned the courage to reach out a hand and place it on the back of her neck. With a pang of sadness, he realised it was the last time he would ever touch her.

Finally, she stopped crying.

'It's probably best I move out now. During the holidays. I can't face it in term time.'

'Why don't we give it one more term and see what happens?'

'Nah, Winkler, I don't think it's going to work out. Let's try to end on a good note.'

He let that sink in for a moment, before replying.

'If this is how you end on a good note, I'd sure hate to end on a bad one.'

They both looked towards the open window, where *The Watergirl's Pitcher* had made such a spectacular exit, in that graceful parabolic arc to the other side of the street. Realising the absurdity of the situation, they broke into laughter.

Winkler had once read that, in times of crisis, the mind focuses on the smallest, most irrelevant details. He now recalled that as a very young boy he'd had the idea that the weather was always either sunny or raining, but never both at once, and his later surprise when he saw a sun shower. Now, as he looked at his soon-to-be-ex, he saw that she was laughing and crying at the same time.

Sonia sniffed, and spoke to him softly.

'Let's remember the good times, Winkler. We had a few laughs.'

She turned and headed for the bedroom. Winkler went straight for the Scotch cupboard and grabbed the bottle. Within an hour, he was passed out on the couch, so drunk that not even Marla herself could enter his dreaming mind.

VIII – Immersion

Winkler's sorrow over Sonia lasted only a little longer than his hangover. Now the schism between them was exposed, their illusory future vanished like morning fog. She was gone in a week, and Winkler immediately changed the locks, then began to set the place up as his own Marla Okadigbo kingdom. He was now free to be himself. Or rather, his new self, for he was transitioning to another state entirely.

In his mind, there was a sound rationale for this. To create the *Watergirl* sequel, the guiding principle was authenticity. Much as he tried to ignore it, his hidden fear was that *The Watergirl's Pitcher* was really a fake, and any close inspection of the work would in time bring that to light. For the sequel he aimed to produce a work with such authenticity of tone it might even drag its predecessor along with it. Who knows, perhaps he could even rewrite *Watergirl* for a second edition? Now Marla was really part of him, he could do the job properly.

The quest required total immersion in the role. First there was the apartment to set up. Winkler hired a car and drove to New York, then gathered as many artefacts of black culture as he could find. Among these were pictures of black icons: politics (Luther-King, Malcolm X, Obama), music (Bessie Smith, BB King, Dr Dre), sport (Michael Jordon, Venus Williams), comedy (Eddie Murphy, Chris Rock), and so on.

He returned to his New Jersey apartment and filled the walls with these pictures, along with some African art. Yet the main space opposite the front door was saved for two items: a large, framed reproduction of *The Watergirl's Pitcher* cover, and a blown up version of the Marla photo, also framed. These took pride of place in his living room.

He now listened only to black music, and read books by black authors. Naturally, too, the focus of his research became a fairly obsessive look at African-American culture and history.

He did it in stages beginning with slavery to the end of the civil war, through the segregation era, civil rights and black power, and on through the decades up to Obama's presidency. This is not to say he fixated only on episodes of conflict; they were just part of his quest to see the big picture.

Throughout this study, he felt Marla around. Her interest was not constant by any means, but came and went with no obvious pattern. Her identity was merged with his, and to some degree, she was the driver. It was *her* fascination with black history and culture that infused his own. Yet, for her, it was not history but a glimpse into the future

He pushed on in the belief that the sought-after authenticity was attainable. Between his research into history, the immersion in black culture, and the 'Marla-izing' of his consciousness, Winkler Jones was no longer the jaded white man who'd written *The Watergirl's Pitcher*, he was Winkler Okadigbo, a creature in transition from one state of being to another.

His yearning for Marla was part spiritual, part intellectual, but inevitably took on a physical dimension. Although it was not his normal habit, one night his desire to embody Marla became overwhelming, and the simplest answer was just a phone call away.

By the time the girl showed up at the door, he'd covered up his more eccentric decorations, including the framed pictures. As it turned out, Leticia was friendly enough, although a little surprised by Jones' intensity. Physically, the girl was no dead ringer for Marla, but they might have been fourth cousins twice removed, and his imagination did the rest.

After she left, he felt the real Marla inside him looking on kindly, not judging or resenting his actions. He wondered if the encounter would be a one off. He'd half-consciously hoped the act might purge him of his odd obsession. No such luck, for he was as entranced as ever. It was all part of the process, part of his Marla-izing. And why not? Obsession had always worked for him in his creative endeavours. He wanted immersion. Total immersion.

Winkler felt sure the sequel would be the most important of his books. His earlier novels had been intelligent thrillers. Page turners with a philosophical subtext, but trivial really, compared to his current work. *Watergirl Two* would be *important*. It was capable of advancing profound social change and unifying America. He would employ every facet of his literary skill, every artifice and power of expression, to deliver the message. Yet it was to Marla, his muse, that he looked for inspiration.

He returned to his conjecture as to plot. Of course, Kamali would have to leave Canadia with all its boring Utopian qualities, and return to the exciting racist dystopia of America in 2055. There, Kamali would lead a *Hunger Games* style rebellion to overthrow the fascist white government. Thus, she who had begun as a slave would end as a queen.

Expecting this plot to pan out fairly predictably, he turned to Marla for its tone. Her spirit would fuel the thrust of the novel. It would be a cry of rage at the plight of her people. As a white man, he could not feel it with any authenticity, so he looked to Marla to provide it.

On he continued with his immersion in black history and culture. He watched a range of historical footage and, through him, Marla watched too. Yet this brought results he hadn't expected. The early twentieth century footage showed poverty and hard times, but in Marla he sensed not rage, but curiosity. The era of the fifties through seventies brought fascination at the social changes. By the time they came to the twenty-first century, her state of mind was astonishment. Marla saw musical megastars like Beyonce, Oprah hosting prime time TV, black sports stars earning millions of dollars, and finally the biggest surprise of all - a black man as president. Marla's state of mind was not rage, but stunned disbelief.

This was not what Winkler was after. Disappointed, he showed her footage of riots, beatings, gangs, thugs, and ghettos. Even this did not produce the required outrage, but a sense of confusion that the images co-existed with the other ones.

Still, as they watched and learned, the plot for book two began slowly to form.

IX – Cracks

That's when the edifice began to crumble.

The first inkling came when a fake Twitter account surfaced. With the handle @therealMarlaOkadigbo, it began posting cryptic messages like 'no such thing as a white lie?' or 'am I the slave or the master?' Not long after that, Steve Cassel made a surprise visit to Winkler's apartment.

Winkler was at work on the sequel, and about to start his second cup of coffee, when the doorbell rang. He looked up in annoyance. His writing flow had just begun and any interruption might derail it. It must be some salesman or other. He stood up to get rid of them, but looked through the peephole and saw his agent. At once, Winkler became aware of his own casual appearance - shorts and an old t-shirt, three days growth - and the state of his apartment. Reluctantly, he opened the door.

'Cass. What's up?'

Cassel pushed past him into the room.

'Have you spoken to anyone? Someone's been asking around. We need to ...'

He broke off in mid-sentence.

'What the fuck, Wink?'

Cassel stared around the apartment with the African art, pictures of black cultural icons, and the giant framed photos of Marla and the *Watergirl* cover.

'Welcome to my world,' said Winkler.

'Are you out of your mind?' his agent said. 'I told you not to tell your girlfriend.'

'Relax, Cass. We broke up ages ago.'

'Who else has seen this?'

'No one comes in here. This is my work space.'

'You're crazy. If anyone sees all this, they'll figure it out. Take it down - now!'

'Not gonna happen. Not if you want book two. I have to get in the right headspace - total residence in Marla-land.'

'Jesus Christ, Winkler. Do you know why I've come here today? Some journo's been sniffing around. Better stay away from the office for a while.'

'Who is it?'

'How would I know? Some wannabe. She's demanding an interview with Marla and I can't shake her off.'

'You think she knows something?'

'How could she? I've kept everything under wraps.'

Cassel cast an angry glance around the room.

'But then I come out here and see *this*!'

Winkler felt obliged to defend himself. He sat down in his favourite armchair.

'Look,' he said. 'Let's get something straight. You're the businessman and you handle the business stuff. I'm the writer and I take care of the creative process. If that means going full-Marla in my workspace, so be it. Once you read book two, you'll see it was worth it. And I assure you - until the book's done, absolutely no one comes in here. Not even the pizza delivery boy.'

Cassel, unconvinced, sat down in the chair opposite.

'What about these messages on Twitter? You're aware of them, right? Someone knows something! Level with me, Wink. Have you told anyone about Marla?'

'Of course not.'

'What about all that research you were doing? Maybe someone twigged what was up. Come on, think!'

Jones leaned back in his chair, staring into space.

'I don't think so. Geez - I hope not.'

'What about when you bought all this crap?' Cassel gave a contemptuous wave of his arm at the home decor. 'Did they deliver it here?'

'Nah. I brought it all back myself.'

'What about the pictures? Where'd you get them framed?'

'Two different shops. See? I'm not a complete dunce.'

Steve Cassel sat there, shaking his head.

'I'm warning you, Wink. If you messed up somehow, don't think I'm gonna bail you out.'

'Thanks Cass. Nice to know you've got my back.'

'Have you finished the new book? The sooner we get it out, the sooner any speculation might drop off.'

'Give me a week or two and you'll have it. I guess it's another rush release?'

'You better believe it. So, soon as it's done, tell me you're gonna rip all this down. Right?'

'Why should I? No one's got this address?'

Cassel snorted.

'There's no such thing as privacy anymore. Someone wants to find you, they will.'

'So, just hypothetically, this journo - what if she does come after me?'

'No comment. That's what you say.'

'And if she does know something?'

'Code Peter: deny, deny, deny. It's a biblical thing.'

'Look Cass - maybe I should just come clean about writing *The Watergirl's Pitcher*. After all, it's still a great book, right?'

Steve Cassel fixed Jones in the spotlight of an icy glare.

'If you want to commit professional suicide, I can't stop you. But don't think for one second I'll be going down with you.'

X – Exposed

True to his word, Winkler finished book two, to which he gave the simple title *The Watergirl's Return*. To celebrate, he flew to LA for some R n R, taking his friend Leticia with him. When they landed back on the east coast a week later, he put her in a taxi, then returned to his apartment alone. He turned the key in the lock, put on some coffee, went to the bathroom, then entered his workroom to catch up on email.

There was a blue light on at the front of his desktop computer. But how? He never left his computer on when he went away. While he was processing this thought, his hand habitually touched the mouse and the dark screen lit up. A Word document was open on the screen, with the simple heading, 'You Bastard!'

Winkler. I can't believe you changed the locks. Thank God Helen was home. She let me climb around from her balcony. (Well, what am I supposed to do when you won't return my calls?) Even then I had to break the damn bathroom window. Thanks for the inconvenience!

All I wanted was the towels and plates my grandmother left me, which I forgot to take. Then when I got inside ...   If I'd found you lying dead on the floor, that wouldn't have been a total surprise, but I certainly didn't expect *this*!

At first I thought someone else had moved in. But no, there were the same crappy old Winkler armchairs and your other junk. Then I saw your stupid *Watergirl's Handjob* book cover framed on the wall and it all started to make sense.

So I turned on your computer. (You really should password it, you know.) I checked your files and there are several drafts of your famous book. That explains your totally weird behaviour, and when I remember how I tossed your masterpiece out the window, it's kind of hilarious really. Sorry to be a bitch, but it is.

Winkler, I don't know whether to laugh or cry. I wanted you to be a success, but WTF !!! Hey, just putting this out there, but did you ever think about maybe being HONEST with me about what you were doing? I know I kind of gave you a hard time about your job, but can you blame me? You hadn't put out a book since we met - what do you expect me to think? I wasn't to know you were writing this thing, so it's a fair assumption for me to think you're sitting on your ass doing nothing.

As for the book itself, I guess you remember my thoughts on that! But, you know, maybe if you had told me about it, I could have given you some input and it would have turned out different somehow? Well Mr Secretive, all that deception is about to blow up in your face, because I can't forgive how you lied to me. I wasted three years of my life on you and I can't get them back. You know I wanted kids, and you wasted my time because you're a liar. Sorry, this is karma, and I am just its instrument.
Sonia

In a state of shock, Winkler immediately went online and checked the news. On the first site he went to, he had only to scroll down the page a little to find not just his identity laid bare, but actual photos of his living room in full colour. While he'd known Sonia had a vindictive streak, he wouldn't have thought she'd go this far. Wrong. Oh so wrong. Stunned, he read through the main article.

Literary Fraud Exposed

For months, journalists have been trying to track down the elusive Marla Okadigbo, author of hit novel *The Watergirl's Pitcher*. There's a reason Marla's been so well hidden. It turns out 'Marla' is actually white, male author, Winkler Jones.

Jones, author of B-list novels *The Shortstop* and *Trade Winds Incorporated*, is believed to be in hiding. His agent, Steve Cassel, fronting the media, made the extraordinary claim to have never met the author of *The Watergirl's Pitcher*.

'I'm as shocked as anyone else. I hope these allegations aren't true, but if they are, they'll be treated with the utmost seriousness by the Steve Cassel Literary Agency. All I know is we got this great manuscript in the mail and, despite numerous attempts, I could never get Marla to come into the office. I put it down to shyness, so we put the book out in good faith. If it turns out to have been a hoax by one of my clients, there'll be hell to pay, I can assure you of that. We're trying to track down Jones at this moment, so I'm going to give him a message right now. Winkler, if you're out there, get in touch. We need to sort this out.'

Winkler laughed as he read this. 'Well played, Cass.' He reasoned, also, that if Cassel had gone to the extent of a public statement, the game was up.

Winkler checked some other news sites. He thought the headlines were rather extreme. 'Slave Book Author Outed as White Supremacist' said one. 'Racist Bestseller Pulled From Sale' said another. Yet the most damning report came in a *New York Times* feature piece.

Literary Blackface

So black activist writer Marla Okadigbo is really a middle class white man living a cushy life in New Jersey? Say it ain't so, Marla.

The news has rocked not just the literary world, but Okadigbo's African-American fans, many of whom refuse to believe it. Yet, as one cynic put it, if Marla Okadigbo didn't exist, someone would have had to invent her. Well - looks like someone did. In the dark days of the Trump presidency and Black Lives Matter, blacks were waiting for a powerful voice of liberation. In *The Watergirl's Pitcher*, they seemed to have found one. A science fiction tale that saw slavery restored in America was exactly the type of empowering tale African-Americans had been crying out for. It turns out to have been a cruel hoax, which has dashed the hopes of a suffering people.

In assessing this scandal, it's hard to know which is

the most egregious crime. Is it the vulgar opportunism of a white guy fleecing the money of hard-working black folks on the back of a literary lie? Is it the shameless cultural appropriation of a black identity? Or the cynical assumption of a female persona to gain feminist sympathies?

It may be none of the above, but the author's deeper intention - the restoration of actual slavery in racist white America. The book is a Trojan horse pretending to rail against slavery when its real aim is to restore it. What else do you expect from a white supremacist?
We might, furthermore, take a closer look at the literary worth of Jones' masterpiece. That it is a bestseller means little, but its laughable nomination for a Pulitzer boggles the mind. I spent the last twenty-four hours re-reading *The Watergirl's Pitcher* and the results weren't pretty.

What exactly is it that scores a Pulitzer these days? Is it the flimsy and melodramatic plot? The cardboard cut out characters? The pretentious, faux-biblical prose that pathetically apes Hemingway and McCarthy? Or is it the shamelessly derivative plunder of respectable works in the science fiction canon? I'll leave it to the Pulitzer committee to figure that out.

But, when all is said and done, there's a yet greater crime in the wings of this literary farce. Apparently there's going to be a sequel. Oh Winkler, say it ain't so.

XI – Betrayed

Just as Winkler finished reading this piece, he turned on his phone to be greeted by the news he had eighty-nine missed calls. Right on cue, the phone rang again. With a mix of hope and dread, he saw Cassel's number come up on the screen. Cass would know what to do. Yet his agent's manner was strangely formal.

'Winkler, I need you to come in to the office.'

'Have you seen the press?'

'What do you think? I'm not going to discuss this on the phone. Just come in right away.'

A couple of hours later, Winkler, wearing a long coat, hat, and dark glasses, walked into the office of the Steve Cassel Literary Agency. He was surprised to see two burly black security guys on the outer doors, and two more inside. When he entered Cassel's office, his agent looked him up and down.

'Take off the coat.'

'Why?'

'And the hat.'

When Jones complied, Cassel picked up the hat and coat and dumped them outside his door.

'Now give me your phone and empty your pockets.'

'For Christ's sake!'

'When you're done, lift up your shirt and take down your pants.'

'What's with the mafia routine?'

'Just do it.'

When Cassel was finally satisfied Jones wasn't wearing a wire, he watched his client pull up his pants.

'Winkler, I regret that the Steve Cassel Literary Agency has unanimously decided we can no longer continue in business. together. Our contract is null and void, as of today.'

'What are you talking about?'

'I'm afraid there's a certain level of trust required for an agent-author relationship. One that you've violated through this unfortunate act of fraud.'

'Say... what?'

'I'm sorry, but reputation is everything in this business. So let's part, and I wish you well in your future endeavours.'

'You rat! I'd never even have written the book without you.'

Steve Cassel looked astonished.

'I wouldn't dream of commissioning a work like that from a white author. Frankly, Winkler, I had no idea you were even a racist, let alone a white supremacist - and it's pretty devastating to think we had one of them in our stable the whole time.'

'Like that, is it? Then guess what, Steve? I'm going to come clean. I'll tell everyone the whole story of how *The Watergirl's Pitcher* was your idea in the first place.'

'Do you have any evidence of that? Any emails, phone records? Any correspondence with this office about your despicable book?'

'Of course not. You were the one who told me not to leave a paper trail.'

'In that case, Jones, I advise you to cease and desist. If you persist in these slanderous allegations, you can add a lawsuit to your troubles.'

'I could kill you.'

'No doubt you saw the security boys on the door. Some fine young African-American boys. I hired them only yesterday. A nod from me, and they'll be happy to give your sorry white ass the beating it deserves.'

'Unbelievable.'

Cassel paused and looked thoughtful.

'Now look, Jones, I'm going to give you some advice. You've caused our agency a lot of embarrassment. I am personally dismayed, and it's going to take quite a while to restore trust in the Steve Cassel Literary Agency. The repair job's only just begun. I've given my personal promise to sign up three new African-American authors this very week. I've also publicly suggested that all royalties from your odious book go to poor single mothers in urban communities. I can't force you to do that, but I suggest you comply.'

'You are Satan.'

Cassel smiled.

'Look, Winkler, it's nothing personal. Publishing's a funny game. Sometimes you win, sometimes you lose, and sometimes both at once. I'm going to give you some advice. It's a long road back for you from here, but hang in and you can make it.'

'Oppression's nothing new to me, Steve. It's what I was born to. I'm used to suffering.'

Cassel frowned.

'I wouldn't play the victim card, Wink. They won't buy it.'

'I don't mean Winkler Jones. I mean my other life.'

'What are you talking about?'

'To be honest, I'm not angry with you, Cass. Not really. After all, you introduced me to Marla. She's part of me now.'

'No she isn't,' said Cassel. 'That's the whole point. Now, before we part, let me give you a tip. If you want to come back from this, get down on your hands and knees and beg the forgiveness of the American public. It's the first step in your road to redemption - and if you're patient, one day there might once again be a Winkler Jones.'

Winkler adopted a strangely beatific expression.

'I no longer relate to that name. In fact, I no longer identify as a man. Or as white. I feel inside my true identification is that I'm black and female.'

Steve Cassel looked puzzled, then thoughtful. Finally he smiled.

'Winkler Jones, you've got balls. You're really going to play a card out of left field like that? Ha ha. Good luck, kid. You'll probably end up tarred and feathered. Then again, you might just pull it off. Who knows, in crazy times like these?'

'Let them oppress me. Let them persecute me. I was born into slavery, and a slave I may die. Yet they will never enslave my soul.'

Cassel raised his eyebrows.

'Right. Well, good luck with that. I'd say we're done here, so I'll say it once more for old times' sake - and this time I really mean it. Winkler Jones, get the hell outta here before I call the cops!'

XII – Resurrection

Winkler snuck home late at night, packed a suitcase and his laptop, then drove his hire car through the night. At 8am, he checked into the Apollo Grand Hotel in Philadelphia and slept through the day, waking as night fell to begin his work.

This was no cowardly escape but a strategic retreat. He'd decided to rewrite the *Watergirl* sequel and put it out, regardless of any public outcry. For the next four weeks, he wrote through the night, lived off room service, and emerged only in the small hours to use the hotel pool and gym, both of which were deserted at those times.

At last, the book was done. *The Watergirl's Return*. With no publisher willing to touch him, he released it himself as an e-book. He knocked up a quickie website and offered the book for free download.

In the meantime, he'd been keeping an eye on the firestorm caused by the scandal. It had flared up briefly, making the mainstream press as well as the alternative media on YouTube. There was some confusion as to how to interpret the whole event. The left wing attacked him mercilessly as a member of the alt-right. The right wing saw him as a prankster exposing the gullibility and victim-mentality of the left.

He'd also become the go-to whipping boy for late night TV hosts, one of whom was the star of *The Tim Tucker Show*. Tucker had the usual mix of surface charm, selective outrage, and politically acceptable wit. He'd been lampooning Winkler all week from the safety of his late night timeslot. Eventually, Jones tweeted to him 'Want to hear the real story? Invite me on your show and I'll tell all.'

It didn't take long for the offer to be accepted, and the spot was booked for the next Tuesday night. The day before the show, Winkler returned to New York and checked into a hotel. He slept most of the day. Towards evening he woke, showered, dressed and made his way to the studio.

He was taken to the guestroom just offstage, from where he watched Tim Tucker's introduction. Tucker, spruce as ever, wore a dark grey suit that matched his hair and a blue tie that matched his eyes. A handsome white guy in his mid-forties, he was looking to camera with the same smile that had made his journey through life a bit smoother.

'For anyone who's been in a coma the last few weeks, let me bring you up to speed on our next guest. *The Watergirl's Pitcher* was this year's smash hit novel. A sci-fi tale about the return of slavery in America, it was seen as a protest about systemic racism. At least, it was when we thought the author was a young African-American woman named Marla Okadigbo.

Then we found out Marla doesn't exist. The real author's a white man, Winkler Jones. So who is this guy? Is he a conman? A prankster? A white supremacist? Tonight you're going to find out exclusively on *The Tim Tucker Show*. Ladies and gentlemen, please welcome Marla Oka... sorry, Winkler Jones!'

Winkler walked onstage to a mixed reception of applause and boos. He shook hands with Tucker and sat down in the chair to Tucker's right.

'There goes a brave man,' said Tucker.

Confused, Jones looked around, trying to locate him. The audience laughed, their initial hostility softening a touch.

'I mean you, Winkler,' said Tucker. 'You've got some front coming on here. You must be the most hated man in America.'

'Hate's nothing new to me, Tim.'

'So it seems,' said Tucker. 'Apparently your vision for America is for every white family to own a black slave.'

'Ever heard of fiction? Just because it's in the book doesn't mean it should happen.'

'Then why write it?'

'When Orwell wrote *1984*, did he want a real life totalitarian regime?'

'I guess not. I'm no author so I won't presume your motivations. There's sure been a ton of speculation since this thing broke. Winkler, you have the floor. Why'd you do it?'

'It's simple, Tim. I wanted to highlight the plight of black America.'

'By depicting them as slaves?'

'It seemed to strike a chord.'

'It's pretty edgy stuff. Did you ever think about putting the book out under your own name?'

'I did.'

'But what right do you, as a white man, have to speak for African-Americans?'

'That answers your previous question.'

'Does it?'

'It's all about perceptions. As Marla Okadigbo, I was a black hero. As Winkler Jones, I'm a white supremacist. But not one word changed in the entire book.'

Unsure how to respond, Tim Tucker used one of his go-to moves. He turned to camera and raised an eyebrow. On cue, there were a few titters from the audience. Tucker turned back to his guest.

'So - are you a white supremacist?'

'Why would I betray my people like that?'

'What do you mean *your people?*'

'What makes you think I'm white?'

There were some rumbles from the audience. Tucker turned to the camera with a half-smirk.

'I'm looking at you, Winkler. You're white. You're a white American man.'

'What makes you think I'm a man?'

There were more rumbles, louder now. Tucker went full-smirk.

'Winkler Jones, you playing with me?'

'I no longer identify with that name.'

Tucker laughed out loud.

'You want me to call you Marla?'

'That is my preference. I no longer identify as a man, and when you call me Winkler it makes me really uncomfortable.'

'You mean to say... you're trying to tell me something?'

'Yes, Tim, I'm transgender. You got a problem with that?'

The smirk vanished. A small alarm bell went off in Tucker's mind, prompting him to silence. Then he spoke.

'This some gender dysphoria thing?'

Winkler looked offended.

'Gender dysphoria is not a *thing*, Tim. I'm sure some of your viewers would appreciate you choosing your words a little more sensitively.'

'I'm sorry, uh... Marla. Do you want to talk about it?'

'I'm happy to. After all, I read your network's inclusiveness policy, which guaranteed it was a safe space for diverse genders and minorities. That's why I selected your program as my platform for coming out.'

By now rather alarmed, Tim Tucker sat up straight in his host's chair.

'Of course. I didn't realise because, well, you know...'

He reached for a glass of water. Winkler let him stew for a bit before replying.

'Because I look like a man? Because I'm wearing a business suit like any white man going to the office? Let's be clear on this, Tim. My clothing doesn't define my gender identity any more than my body does. You want me to wear a dress like some gaudy caricature? Sorry, not sorry. If I choose to wear a clothing archetype monopolised by the male gender, that's my right as a woman.'

'OK, Marla. Point taken. So, have you, uh... had the surgery?'

'I'm waiting for some progress in the gender pay gap. Do you realise women make up only five percent of surgeons? Until there's gender parity in the medical profession, I wouldn't dream of getting it done. In the meantime, I'm sure your audience will take it on trust that, yes, I've got a penis.'

There were some titters from the gallery. Tucker looked towards his producer, just offstage, wondering if she would bail him out. No such luck.

'Of course,' Winkler continued. 'My possession of male genitalia doesn't define me. It's what I feel inside. I'm proud to identify as a woman, and I always will. In no way does my penis make me a man.'

'OK, Marla. I guess you've got a point, and I respect your opinion as a woman. But the other thing, you know, the...'

Winkler leaned forward aggressively.

'My race, Tim? My race? Is that what you're alluding to?'

'Well, yeah,' Tucker said timidly. 'No offence, but... you're white, aren't you?'

Winkler fell back as if slapped, then seemed to be about to burst into tears. He took his face in his hands.

'Sorry, Marla,' said Tucker. 'I meant no offence.'

'When I came on your program, I had no idea I'd be subjected to racial slurs.'

'I didn't mean to imply anything.'

'Hate speech - and on national TV. Who's the racist now?'

Tucker, by now somewhat rattled, went into damage control. 'I'm no racist, Marla. I swear.'

'Really, Tim? How many African-American women did you have on your show last week?'

'Hell, I don't know. I'll check the guest list if you like. We want to give all minorities a voice.'

Winkler dabbed at his own tears, then magnanimously reached out a hand.

'Don't worry, Tim. I don't think you're a racist. I'm just trying to bring some awareness to the issue of racial dysphoria.'

'Is that... ?'

'That's right - the racial version of sexual dysphoria. I'm transgender and I'm also transracial. Just because I look white on the outside doesn't mean I feel white on the inside. People need to realise that.'

'Uh, right. Like that woman, Rachel D...'

'Yeah her. Rachel D. Exactly.'

'So, if I'm hearing you right, you're actually a black woman.'

'That is correct. And you, Tim, are a white male. So - you want to ask me again if I'm a white supremacist?'

'No, and I apologise if it came across as offensive. I guess this changes everything. *The Watergirl's Pitcher* really is a protest about the condition of black America in 2020.'

'It is, but *The Watergirl's Pitcher* is only half the message. The other half will come in the sequel, *The Watergirl's Return*. Here's a scoop for your viewers. For the next twenty-four hours, it's available as an ebook for free download on my new website.'

'Wow - a sequel already? That's exciting. So what's it about?'

'I'd love to tell you all about it, but you know what? I think I'll get Marla to do that.'

Tucker, confused, took another sip of water.

'But... you're Marla,' he said. 'Isn't that what you just told us?'

'Sure, Tim, but there's Marla, and there's Marla-Marla. Before I go on, I've got to give you a trigger warning. Are you ready for me to blow your mind?'

Tucker glanced desperately at his producer, who gave him the thumbs up.

'OK,' he managed 'Go ahead.'

Winkler paused theatrically, and stared into space.

'You believe in spirits, Tim? Believe in the soul?'

'Maybe,' said Tucker, cautiously.

'When I began writing *The Watergirl's Pitcher*, I was Winkler Jones, a white American man. Then somehow, somewhere along the way, Marla came to me. A spirit, but not so very long ago, she walked this Earth just like you and me. She was born into slavery and died in it. But in her life, she prayed and she had faith. Don't know if she prayed to Jesus, or the African gods - maybe both - but she prayed that if ever she was gonna be born again, she'd be born into a world without slavery. Her prayers were granted, Tim. She was born again, inside me.'

'You mean... she's here now?'

'She's here.'

'A black slave girl?'

'As sure as I sit before you.'

'Let me get this straight. You're saying there's an actual black slave from the nineteenth century inside you?'

'She thinks my thoughts, she feels what I feel. She's looking at you now.'

Tucker shook his head.

'That's one hell of a story. Don't take this the wrong way, but can you prove it? Can she talk?'

'You better believe it.'

'I don't mean you, Marla, but, you know...'

'Marla-Marla? Oh yeah, she can talk. That's the *real* reason I came on your show.'

'Does she have a message for us?'

'She's got a message for all her people.'

Tucker gave one last glance at his producer. This time she gave him both thumbs up.

'OK, Marla. We can't wait to hear your message. We're going to cut to a commercial break, then you have the floor - and all America's waiting to hear it.'

After an extra long ad break, *The Tim Tucker show* came back on air.

'Here we go,' said Tucker. 'We're about to hear from Marla. The real Marla.'

He turned to his guest. 'You ready?'

'Give me a moment,' said Winkler

Winkler closed his eyes. He slumped back in the chair, his head lolling to the side. Nearly a minute passed, til Tucker was getting antsy at the dead air time. Then, just as Tucker was checking his watch, Winkler sat up straight. He smiled, then spoke in a voice quite unlike his own. It was a feminine voice yet deep, with a strangely archaic accent. At first, the words were unclear, as if a new mind had taken over the body and was trying to understand how it worked. The stream of words came out half formed and garbled, then slowly came into focus.

Tucker sat bolt upright.

'Marla?' he said. 'Is that you?'

There was a pause and then the voice spoke.

'My name ain't Marla ... you kin call me that if you want.'

Tucker, looking a little spooked, decided to roll with it.

'Uh, when were you born?'

'Born Louisiana, 1793. Died 1820.'

'How did you die?'

'My baby done kill me.'

'Huh?'

'By mistake.'

'Oh. You mean you died in childbirth?'

'Yeh.'

'Why did you come back?'

'To see your world.'

'Marla, do you have a message for us? For your people that are alive today?'

'Yeh, I got a message. My message to y'all afore I go back.'

'You're leaving? Why?'

'My prayers be answered. I done seen your world.'

'Wait, Marla, don't go. Tell us. What is your message to your people?'

There was a long silence. Winkler's body slumped, and his head lolled back again. Then his body jerked up straight, like a marionette pulled by strings.

'My message,' the voice continued, 'is for all my chillen an' I'm a-gonna tell it straight, y'hear?'

There was a long pause. The studio audience was deadly quiet. All round America, people held their breath.

'I was a slave.'

Tucker leaned forward, straining to catch every word. Then the voice spoke again.

'An' you ain't.'

And with that, the body slumped back again in the chair. Tucker leaned forward.

'Wait, Marla. Don't go. Explain yourself. Tell us what it means.'

He stood up and shook Winkler by the shoulders. Winkler sat up groggily, rubbing his eyes.

'What happened?'

Tim Tucker looked angry, like he'd been cheated.

'Is that you, Winkler?' he said. 'Bring back Marla. Bring her back now.'

Winkler stared into empty space, as if listening for something. At last he spoke.

'She's gone.'

XIII – *The Watergirl's Return*

That week, the e-book sequel to *The Watergirl's Pitcher* was downloaded over a hundred thousand times. Here is some information from the Wikipedia entry that was later created.

The Watergirl's Return - Plot

In the world of 2055, Kamali returns to the USA and holes up at the secret rebel base in Ohio. She plans to unite minority groups all over the country and lead an uprising against the white fascist government.

However, the rebel scientists have a more ambitious plan. Using secret time travel technology, they aim to go back to 2018 and stop the nuclear explosion that caused the breakdown of society in the first place.

Complicating the mission, the identity of the bombers in 2018 is not clear. They're assumed to be either North Korean operatives, members of ISIS, or far right extremists. Kamali volunteers for the mission. Her brief is to return to 2018, find out who is responsible and stop them, thus preventing the war and the developments that saw the return of black slavery.

Kamali arrives in 2018 a month before the explosion date, November 8th. There she learns that the bombers are not foreign agents or the far right, but members of AFAR, a left wing extremist group obsessed with identity politics. In alliance with Black Lives Matter, AFAR plans to blow up the Whitehouse on the second anniversary of Donald Trump's election win. The group has manipulated a trio of brilliant young scientists into building a nuclear bomb.

On the night before November 8th, Kamali attends a secret meeting of AFAR, having gained their trust due to her status as a black woman. She makes an impassioned plea, telling them she's from the future and that the bombing will lead to a new era of slavery. 'I've seen real oppression,' she says. 'Your world is a Utopia compared to mine. Through your hatred, you will destroy it. Hate doesn't work. You'll only destroy yourselves and everything you have.'

The members of AFAR listen, shocked and disgusted. Then the chanting begins. Liar! Uncle Tom! Nazi! They surround Kamali and beat her to death.
The next night, they successfully blow up the Whitehouse, leading to the collapse of America, the rise of a totalitarian white government, and the return of slavery.

Wikipedia – Reception

The Watergirl's Return received mixed reviews. Dismissed as 'both an alt-right propaganda tract and a shameless *Terminator* rip off,' the book also won praise as 'a deceptively simple call for peace,' and 'a critique of the cancerous identity politics hate-cult that has crippled American universities.'

Soon after publication the author, Winkler Jones, left America to work as a freelance author at an unknown location.

XIV – Postscript

Winkler Jones sat in a deckchair, on a beach somewhere in the South Pacific. As a boy, his favourite book had been *Treasure Island*. At the end of that story, the pirate John Silver escaped his captors and retired to an unknown port with his 'old negress.' Winkler had done much the same with his own lover. She wasn't Marla, but she was the best he could find in *this* world.

Although he lived under an assumed name, he always published under his *own* name, Winkler Jones, and the more frank and clear his opinions, the better. It's what people expected now. Marla Okadigbo had given him that license. So, although he lived in the tropics, he kept an eye on world events. As he watched from a distance the last throes of Western civilisation, he chronicled its idiotic suicide as it strangled itself through lies, cowardice, and myopia.

Winkler didn't think his writing would change anything. He saw himself as merely a violinist on the Titanic, giving people a merry tune as the ship went down. His books sold better now than ever. It was no surprise that Steve Cassel had been back in touch, trying to get a share of the spoils. Winkler always deleted his emails unread. Still, he bore Cassel no ill will. He - along with the faithless Sonia - had played a part in his journey.

The Watergirl's Pitcher; The Watergirl's Return. Could there be a third book in the trilogy? He sometimes regretted killing off Kamali in Book Two, but it was too late now. Perhaps the third book would only come when he met up with Marla in the afterlife. Occasionally, he thought he sensed her around. A rustle in the palm trees; a sea breeze; a tropical fragrance. Then he'd turn back to Leticia and take her hand. If you can't be with the one you love, love the one you're with.

The Golden Rainbow of Love

I

One cold morning in Autumn, a young woman walked into a graveyard. She was a petite woman of about thirty, fair skinned, with dark hair tied back in a bun. Conservatively dressed in a trim grey coat and navy scarf over a white blouse, she might have just stepped off a London bus on the way to the office. Instead, she was here to visit her sister's grave.

Sylvia Scott's visit was long overdue. She'd been putting it off, but facing it was the only way to find closure and move on - for when it came to Eliza, so much had been left unsaid. Indeed, as she walked through the grassy fields of Hurlstone Cemetery in West Sussex, her mind was full of memories.

They'd been typical sisters, playing and squabbling through the years as siblings do: sharing a bedroom at first, fighting over toys, running over the sand on seaside holidays. When little sister, Imogen, arrived five years after Sylvia, they'd taken turns raising her too. Then, in teenage years, a succession of love interests and fleeting melodramas had kept them busy. Liz, Syl, and Immy, the three sisters.

A stranger passing this demure young woman would not have guessed at her lively girlhood, for she had the sober air of the bereaved. Sylvia walked down long paths between rows of graves. Head bowed in mourning, she passed by a copse of trees and rounded a corner, until at last she reached a familiar part of the graveyard. She'd been here once before, but had not lingered. The loss had been too fresh. Still, one cannot delay these things forever.

There was the gravestone, so white and new compared to those around it. The others, in varying shades of grey, were monuments to griefs of decades, even centuries, past. Eliza's gravestone rose up from the ground, ending in a smoothly rounded curve at the top. Slowly, Sylvia approached the sombre memorial, reading the stone's inscription in all its gothic finality.

> Eliza Scott
> 1984-2016
> Weep not that she is gone
> Rejoice that she has been

The surprise came once again, a recurring aftershock. To think it was Eliza - always so assertive, so in control - to be the one cut down by a freak accident. It made no sense. Sylvia sighed. All the things she should have said but hadn't - now all she could do was say them to a grave.

Sylvia took a look around to the left, the right, and over her shoulder. Then, satisfied she was alone, she reached into her handbag. She took out a bottle, full to the brim with a golden elixir, the hue and consistency of a finely distilled Scotch whisky. And indeed, a whisky bottle it was, full size, but just small enough to fit in her handbag. She'd had to tilt the bottle slightly upwards to squeeze it in - all the better not to spill the contents.

A passer-by may have inferred that the young woman, in her grief, sought solace in the warm fires of alcohol, and would have forgiven her indulgence at the unseemly hour of eleven in the morning. For such are life's sorrows that at certain times one must look the other way.

Sylvia unscrewed the lid from the bottle and poured half the contents over her sister's gravestone. It made a conspicuous wet patch on the top and down the front of the stone. Then, at last, she spoke.

'*That's* what you get for unfriending me on Facebook!'

II

Oh. What a strange remark for a mourner to make. For what indeed had Sylvia dispensed upon Eliza's grave? Was it Scotch whisky as some kind of holy water blessing? Was it perhaps apple juice, a refreshment of the same colouration? Alas, it was neither, but another liquid that is a by-product of those beverages. One that is produced without effort by the human body, which indeed Sylvia had produced *herself* over the past twenty-four hours in her own home, transferred carefully to the whisky bottle for camouflage, then carried onto the bus in her handbag. Good Lord, she had doused her sister's grave with piss!

We can only speculate on what kind of twisted psychology would inspire so profane an act. What state of 'sibil war' could produce such a grievance between fair sisters? We are about to find out.

Sylvia had always possessed a vivid imagination and now, in her mind, she saw Eliza's ghost rise up from the grave. She looked just as she had when Sylvia last saw her. Tall, querulous, rather haughty. She was still wearing the same old specs too, so either the afterlife hadn't improved her eyesight or - more likely, one would think - the spectre was projected from Sylvia's own thoughts. If so, Syl must have been imagining her reactions too, for Eliza looked coldly enraged - as, to be fair, one would after what had been done to her last resting place. The phantom rose up and stood behind the gravestone, arms folded, and fixed her living sister with an angry look. Sylvia, held up the bottle - still half-full - in defiance.

'What do you think of *that* then, Lizzy!'

Eliza's ghost said nothing, but merely maintained that lofty stare.

'Not that we were ever that close,' Sylvia continued. 'But

family is family. To be cut off like that, and not a word of warning. No, I just wake up one day and all your Facebook posts are gone. Blocked, I am. Blocked! And no idea why. Oh yes, I sat around for a while, racking my brain over what awful crime I'd committed this time. Did I insult your home decor? Did I kick your cat? Was it something I said?'

Sylvia began pacing back and forth in front of the grave.

'And clearly it was one of your Royal Decrees - because Imogen unfriended me too. Imagine that. You turned my own little sister against me. I tried to let it go. Tried to put it down to one of your passing moods. That's just Lizzy, I said. She'll get over it. Then a month later, no phone call on my birthday. Well... '

Sylvia spun around to face Eliza's ghost.

'I wasn't even that upset,' she yelled. 'Don't flatter yourself! It's the disrespect, that's all. So I blanked you myself and tried to pretend I never had a sister. It would have been fine too, but for one thing.'

The ghost stared stonily back at her as she continued.

'I just wanted to know why. Looking back, I wonder why it seemed so important, but you know me - I never *could* let anything go, could I? That's why I sent the email.'

Sylvia raised the bottle in anger towards her sister.

'And that's how you won. Imagine - me, grovelling to you. Look what you'd turned me into - one of those pathetic girls sucking up to the in-crowd. *You* did that to me.'

Sylvia leaned forward, scowling at the apparition.

'So - did you give me the courtesy of an answer? Did you apologise and say it was all a misunderstanding? No, all I got was a message from your secretary. Your secretary! Far be it from the great Eliza Scott to perform such a lowly task herself! Oh no - you're way too high and mighty for that. And the message, one miserable sentence. I know it off by heart - not really a big ask, memorising that one. *Dear Sylvia, This is to confirm that you were unfriended on Facebook on December 27th. Regards, Patricia, assistant to Ms. Scott.*

Sylvia tossed back her head and laughed wildly.

'Isn't that you to a tee! Your arrogance, your complete lack of manners and respect. And you know what, Eliza? A year later when I heard about your accident, I never shed a tear. Oh yes, I was shocked. Of course I was. After all, unlike you, I'm a human being. But you want to know my first words when I got off the phone with dear old Mummy? *Good.* I said. *Good! Serves her right!'*

Sylvia laughed again, even more wildly.

'I didn't even go to the *funeral.* They tried to make me, but I refused. I had a 'prior commitment,' you know. Some vacuuming, I think it was. Terribly urgent. Because if you think you can treat me like that and I'm going to show up at your funeral and talk about how wonderful you are... well, you can forget it! Mummy wasn't thrilled. But I said I'd make peace with you my own way, in my own time. And here we are, just like I promised. So let's finish the job, shall we, Lizzy? Here's the rest of the *peace* I'm going to make with you!'

Sylvia lifted the bottle and prepared to tip the rest of the urine all over the gravestone. Yet so engrossed in the little scene had she been, she'd failed to notice the arrival of long time family friend and town vicar, the honourable Stephen Brooking, who was standing right behind her. A tall, bespectacled, silver-haired man in his fifties, Vicar Brooking was dressed in his Sunday best like he'd just stepped out of the pulpit. He took off his glasses and squinted.

'Good Heavens - Sylvia. Is that you?'

'Oh... Vicar.' She spun around and snapped back to the real world. 'What are you doing here?'

'I've just finished a service. I was strolling back to the car when I heard a commotion. Turned out to be you. Who were you talking to?'

Sylvia floundered for a moment, white-faced, wondering how long the man had been standing there. She placed the whisky bottle on the ground next to the gravestone, hoping he wouldn't see it.

'I was just... chatting to Eliza,' she said, slowly edging away from the bottle.

Vicar Brooking looked at the headstone and nodded soberly.

'Of course. Dreadful tragedy. I'm so sorry for your loss.'

Sylvia inferred, with a sigh of relief, that the vicar had not picked up the finer details of her rant. Yet now the man's brow furrowed.

'It must be nearly a year. Or is it two? My memory's not what it was, but if I'm not mistaken, you weren't at the funeral. Were you abroad?'

Sylvia considered accepting this ready-made excuse, then realised it might be exposed next time the vicar spoke to her mother.

'Oh no, Vicar. I was... too upset. I couldn't face it.'

Reverend Brooking reached out and patted her shoulder.

'Quite understandable. Grief affects us all in different ways. We must each find our own path through the mourning process. With faith and the forbearance of the Lord, we can move through our sorrow and attain peace of mind.'

Sylvia nodded earnestly, then with a mild sense of alarm, noticed the vicar wrinkling his nose. At the same time, she saw him cast a querying look at the half-full bottle of Scotch beside the grave, then at the gravestone with its rather obvious wet patch. Sylvia's imagination was still vividly at work, and in her mind she continued to see Eliza's ghost lurking behind the gravestone. Acting out Sylvia's unease, the apparition was pointing at the bottle, trying to subliminally draw the vicar's attention to it, and all the while smirking at her sister's discomfort. Searching for a distraction, Sylvia raised a theological dilemma.

'But why would God take her so young?' she said. 'I don't understand.'

'The Lord's ways are ever mysterious,' Brooking intoned, slipping with ease into his preaching manner. 'Bitter are the tears shed by the living, but if Eliza were here now before us, a radiant angel accepted unto God, she would no doubt assure us Heaven's peace is everlasting.'

Eliza's ghost pointed a finger at the side of her own head and rotated it in a 'cuckoo' gesture.

Despite herself, Sylvia felt in danger of erupting into nervous laughter. As the vicar carried on his pompous spiel, she could feel it tickling her.

'Your sister's grace and moral character was well known,' he droned on.

A laugh exploded from Sylvia. She quickly turned it into a cry of anguish, threw her hands to her face and attempted to sob. The vicar turned away respectfully while she composed herself.

'There, there, my child. It will do you good to purge yourself of these sorrows.'

'Thank you, Reverend,' came Sylvia's muffled voice from behind her hands. 'Your words have comforted me. If you had not arrived when you did, I may have lost my faith.'

Eliza's ghost put one finger to her mouth and made gagging gestures. Unseeing, Vicar Brooking's face took on a look of smug satisfaction.

'I am merely a vessel, my child, for He who works through me. Glad am I to do His work, whatever it may be.'

'Thank you, Vicar. And now you have guided me through this spiritual crisis, perhaps I should take my leave.'

'Of course, my dear, and I would be most gratified to see you at church this Sunday.'

Even as he said this, Reverend Brooking was looking askance at the scene before him, as if some small subliminal detail were bothering him. He frowned and wrinkled his nose, as he'd been unconsciously doing the whole time. Then, eyeing the wet patch on the gravestone, he took three steps towards it and picked up the whisky bottle from the ground.

'I say, Sylvia, have you been drinking?'

It seemed best to admit it.

'Oh, you know. Just a drop.'

'Good heavens. The bottle's half-empty. That much intoxicating liquor before lunch is rather concerning.'

'I was upset. That's all.'

'Even so. I mean, really.'

Sylvia, summoning her teenage self and lingo, pointed at the grave in faux outrage.

'Hello? My sister's dead. Know what I mean?'

Brooking was unconvinced.

'Do you have a problem with the stuff? Perhaps we should have a chat.'

'Look, I don't have a problem, alright? Just give me that bottle.'

The vicar tut-tutted.

'Oh dear. That's right out of the textbook. You've no idea how often I've heard those words.'

He held up the bottle and squinted, apparently bothered by its appearance.

'Rather an odd colour, I must say.'

'Give me that bottle. It's mine.'

'Something doesn't add up here.'

Vicar Brooking made a move to unscrew the bottle top, as if to sniff the contents. With a desperate cry, Sylvia sprang at him and snatched the bottle from his hands. The vicar staggered back a couple of paces. It took him a moment to regain his composure.

'Sylvia! I had no idea you were so far gone. I see why the Lord has guided me here today. Well, you're in luck. I'm facilitating a twelve step next week. Why don't you come along and meet the gang?'

'Oh for God's sake, Vicar! I don't have a drinking problem.'

'I'm afraid your conduct says otherwise.'

'I just wanted to have a drink to get through the ordeal of visiting my sister's last resting place.'

Brooking fixed her with a paternal look.

'I don't want to lecture you, but I've spent a lot of time around alcoholics and, let me tell you, there's always a reason. They had a rotten day at work, or the TV's on the blink, or... they had to visit their sister's grave. I'm afraid we rather frown upon that in the program. It's that whole excuse culture we need to move on from, or nothing's ever going to change.'

The vicar stopped, as if remembering something. Finally it seemed to click into place.

'I say, Sylvia, now I think of it, I do believe you were pouring some of that liquor onto the gravestone. That's what I saw from a distance. Is that what these wet marks are? But it doesn't make sense. I know how jealously alcoholics guard their poison. If you've got a drinking problem, why would you be tipping it all over your poor sister's headstone?'

Sylvia drew in a breath and wondered if there was any escape from this farcical scene. She was still seeing Eliza's ghost, which now adopted a quizzical expression in response to the vicar's query. Sylvia considered fleeing, but reasoned Brooking would then examine the gravestone more closely, which wouldn't be good. She sighed.

'If you must know, Vicar, I confess. I am an alcoholic. When Lizzy died, I made a promise to give up, out of respect for her memory. So every month, I come here with a bottle and tip it on Lizzy's grave as a reminder of my pledge.'

'Oh, I see,' said Brooking. He shrugged. 'I've been running the program for over ten years, and I must say that's a first. Tipping liquor on your sister's grave. A rather unique story, come to think of it - and all the more reason you should come and share it with the group.'

'Oh God. If I must.'

'Splendid. We're always looking for inspiration... although, again, it's rather an odd story. Almost too odd.'

He frowned again, and peered suspiciously at the bottle Sylvia was holding.

'I say, give me a look at that whisky? It smells awfully rank. What brand is it? I don't mind a tipple on the odd occasion, but only the decent stuff. Are you in financial straits too, to have to drink such dreadful bilge? Moonshine, is it?'

'Oh well,' said Sylvia. 'It must have passed its use-by date and gone off.'

'Gone off? Whisky doesn't go off, my girl.'

The vicar cast a sudden accusing glance at the wet gravestone.

'I say, hang on a mo. I don't believe that's whisky at all. Give me that bottle at once!'

Sylvia thought of running, then, in a final desperate gambit, unscrewed the lid of the bottle and took a small sip. She tried holding it in her mouth, so as to spit it out again, but under the inquisition of the vicar's gaze, forced herself to swallow. Then, dealing with the awful aftertaste, stood there ashen-faced, grappling with the compulsion to wince.

Brooking, although thrown off a little, still wasn't persuaded.

'The bottle!' he repeated, with slightly less conviction.

Sylvia decided to give her ruse one more shot and if that didn't work, make a run for it. She took another slug from the bottle and drank it down. With a tremendous act of will, she resisted the urge to hurl. She held on gamely - and for a moment, the bluff seemed to have worked.

'Oh, so it is Scotch,' said the vicar. 'But I thought you said you'd given up. I'm afraid that settles it. You're coming to the meeting next week, and I'll not take no for an answer.'

Sylvia, now in danger of losing the arm wrestle with the urge to be violently sick, could only agree.

'Yes, yes,' she gasped, 'I'll be there.'

'Do I have your word?'

'That's what I said. Jesus Christ!'

'Yes, he'll be there too,' said Brooking with a wink. 'Indeed the first step is to admit we've lost control of our lives, and surrender to a higher power.'

And at that moment, the battle was lost. With a cry and a great surge, Sylvia turned away from the Honourable Stephen Brooking and sent a tremendous rainbow of vomit arcing through the air, to land with spectacular precision all over the white marble of Eliza's headstone. Then, realising what she had done, Sylvia could take no more and fled from the scene as fast as she could. And, in her wretched state, the only consoling thought was that the pungent aroma of vomit would be sufficient to overpower the urine, thus covering up her original crime and her considerable public embarrassment.

Or so she thought. For there the story would have ended, if not for the recent installation of security cameras. There are fewer and fewer public areas that go unmonitored these days, and Hurlstone Cemetery was one of the latest to go CCTV. Whether this was done to pick up acts of trespass and vandalism, or put there by optimistic psychic researchers hoping to find signs of supernatural activity, who knows? In any case, a security guard, testing the new equipment, was idly glancing at the footage when he spied the strange incident of Sylvia Scott sending a rainbow arc of vomit all over the white marble of her sister's gravestone.

Through a stroke of luck - or perhaps, some divine intervention - the footage was clear. The public spirited chap passed it on, and from there it was only a matter of time before the story made social media, then the press. Because Vicar Brooking was so beautifully also in shot, Sylvia was even dubbed 'Exorcist Girl,' after the scene in *The Exorcist* where Linda Blair projectile-vomits pea soup onto the priest. Fortunately for Syl, there was no audio on the footage, but when the press found out her identity and connection to the gravestone, they knew they had a winner. *The Daily Mail* ran a story with the headline 'Drunk Woman Vomits on Sister's Grave,' and the story quickly blew up all over the internet.

By the time Sylvia found out, it was too late to do anything but let it blow over. Which it quickly did, of course - but in the meantime, Sylvia gained momentary worldwide fame. In horrified surprise, she watched over and over the mortifyingly clear footage which showed her holding a bottle of Scotch while shouting at her sister's grave, arguing with the vicar, and finally snatching the bottle from his hands, vomiting on the grave, and running off.

Some wit had seen fit to set the scene to *The Exorcist* theme music, which made everything just perfect, didn't it?

As a side effect, the sudden notoriety brought a rush of attention, ranging from some unanswered phone calls from her mother, to several Facebook friend requests from people she hadn't seen since school, and indeed some from people she'd never met.

After three days of the frenzy, there was still one person who hadn't got in touch, and that was her little sister, Imogen. Not that they'd ever been super close. The five year gap, not to mention her blonde hair beside Sylvia's dark, had caused many in the past to express surprise that they were sisters. But as Imogen, having unfriended her along with Lizzy, had something to do with this whole chain of events, Sylvia decided it was about time they had it out.

She arrived at Imogen's house and knocked at the door. After a while, the curtain in a side-window parted and a sleepy looking blonde face peered out. The door opened.

'Look who it is,' said Imogen. 'Exorcist Girl.'

'Don't call me that,' said Sylvia.

'I didn't. It was the press. Oh well, come in.'

Sylvia walked into an untidy living room. Working from muscle memory, Imogen called up some manners and offered her sister a cup of tea.

'Where have you been, anyway?' Imogen said, when they'd sat down. 'Now I think of it, I haven't seen you around for ages.'

Sylvia bristled.

'Now you *think* of it? You've only just noticed?'

'I've been busy.'

'It's been *two years*. It's nice to know the gaping hole my absence leaves in people's lives.'

'Well, where'd you go?'

'I didn't *go* anywhere. You unfriended me on Facebook!'

'Did I?'

'Don't deny it.'

'Now you mention it, I do sort of remember.' She paused. 'Don't tell me you've been in a tiff all this time over that.'

Sylvia took a moment to ponder the indignity of something she'd been het up over, being dismissed as trivial. You would *expect*, she thought, that losing one sister might have made Imogen value the other. Apparently not.

Imogen seemed to sense something more was expected of her.

'I don't really use Facebook anymore,' she said. 'So it's not like it's a big deal.'

'Aaaargh! I could strangle you sometimes.'

Sylvia picked up a cushion to throw, but restrained herself.

'Why'd you even unfriend me?' she said. 'I just want to know why, that's all. What did I do to deserve that?'

'Gee, Syl, keep your bra on. It was Lizzy told me to.'

'Really?' Sylvia nodded grimly. 'I knew it.'

'Oh yes, she was in one of her moods, you know. I assumed it would blow over. Then there was the accident.'

Imogen thought for a moment, putting two and two together.

'Is *that* why you weren't at the funeral?'

'Yes! It might seem ever so trivial, but obviously some people don't understand how hurtful it is to be cut off like that by your own sisters.'

'If it means that much to you, let's friend up again. OK?'

'It's a bit late now.'

'Suit yourself, Syl. Gee, all this over some silly old TV show.'

'What do you mean?'

'That's why you got unfriended. Remember last time we all went over to Mummy's for Christmas?'

'Just before you cut me off?'

'It's kind of dumb, now I think of it. Anyhow, we were all

sitting around on Christmas Day, killing time. Some old 1970s sitcom came on TV and you laughed at it.'

'And?'

'That's all. You laughed at it.'

'It's a comedy. That's what you're supposed to do - right?'

'Oh no, Syl. It was one of those really sexist ones that they had in the seventies. Like, the one with the sideburns guy living with two girls.'

'*Man About the House*?'

'I don't know what it's called, Syl. My friends and I don't watch anything more than two years old. But actually, now I remember. It was that one in the department store - Grace Brothers.'

'You mean *Are You Being Served*?'

'The one with the woman talking about her pussy all the time. And the camp sales assistant, and the straight guy sexually harassing the young girl in the women's department. Anyhow, that old sexist seventies humour didn't go down too well with Lizzy. She would have turned it off except Mummy was enjoying it. But when she saw you laughing too, she stormed out and went home.'

'That's not fair, Imogen. I was probably drinking at the time. It was Christmas Day. I can't have engaged in consensual laughter if I was affected by alcohol. Besides, I was just humouring Mummy.'

Imogen shrugged.

'You think I care what you laugh at? Please. But the next day Lizzy rang up all huffy and told me to freeze you out. She said, if Sylvia thinks gender stereotypes and sexual harassment are funny, she'll soon find out different.'

Sylvia was quiet for a minute. Finally she spoke, in tones of astonishment.

'Do you really mean to say it was all over that?'

'Looks like it.'

'You mean I stayed away from my sister's funeral, had all those sleepless nights, pissed on her grave, and got famous as Exorcist Girl just because of some old seventies sitcom?'

'Pissed on her grave?'

'Ah, I mean vomited. Slip of the tongue.'

'I suppose when you think about it, it's kind of silly, don't you think? Anyway, Syl, why don't we put it behind us? I've only got one sister left now, and that's you. Maybe we can even turn a negative into a positive. Maybe it's all for the best what happened. Let's try and see your vomit as a symbol.'

'A symbol of what?'

'Let's not see it as a big arc of projectile vomit. Look at it as a bridge. A golden rainbow bridge of love that brought us back together. I mean, even Lizzy would want us to move on, don't you think?'

'I don't know.'

'Just think. If you hadn't barfed on her grave, it never would have gone viral. Then you wouldn't have come to see me today to have it out. Then we might never have reconciled.'

'Wow, Imogen, maybe you're right! Let's try to see it as a bottle half-full not half-empty. We can't bring her back, but at least we can salvage something from what came after. At the end of the day, a viral vomit video's brought us back together.'

'Oh Syl, let's never fall out again! Let's be sisters forever and honour Eliza's memory.'

Suddenly the two sisters were embracing, their estrangement ended, and they cried tears of joy at such a wonderful reconciliation.

V

A few weeks later, there they were - the whole family sitting around for Christmas dinner, with a long time family friend as the guest of honour.

'I say,' said Vicar Brooking, raising a glass of Scotch. 'I propose a Christmas toast to family and the holy spirit.'

'Thank you, Stephen,' said Sylvia's mother. 'It's wonderful we're all back together again.'

'Hear, hear, Mummy,' said Sylvia. 'And just think - if I hadn't vomited on Eliza's grave, it would never have happened.'

'The Lord works in mysterious ways,' intoned Vicar Brooking with a wink.

'The golden rainbow of love brought us together,' said Sylvia.

'God bless us every one,' said Imogen, quoting Dickens.

Then, truth be told, they all got a bit jolly, and a fine time was had by all. After dinner, they were channel surfing and some old seventies sitcom came on. They were just tipsy enough to have a guilty laugh or two. Mind you, there was some mysterious banging and clattering, such as the gullible might ascribe to a poltergeist - but more rational minds knew it was just a Christmas wind rattling through the town.

Ghost Squad

I

Sometimes being a millionaire just ain't enough.

It's said that lottery winners, after an initial spike of happiness, return to the same levels of contentment they had before. If they weren't that happy to start with, chances are they'll be miserable again before long, even if they do manage to hang on to their wealth. Some of them blow that and all!

Helena Bentley wasn't a lottery winner, except in the genetic stakes. She'd been born with such striking looks she was a supermodel by eighteen. Milky skin in fine-sculpted features, offset by dark-chocolate hair that looked good long or short (it was long at the moment), and eyes that shimmered like an LA pool on a summer day. It was as if some portrait painter had been given an ordinary supermodel and told to 'pretty her up a bit.' Such beauty brought in a few pounds, Euros, and American dollars as well. But sooner or later, everything gets old. By the time she turned twenty-two, the demon boredom was rattling her cage. I mean, how many nightclubs, shops, and tropical islands can you go to before the tedium of permanent Christmas sets in?

When she got back to London she set up some face time with Webster, her manager.

'I'm so over it, Webs,' she said, sprawling on a chaise longue in his office. 'I've sort of done it all, know what I mean?'

'Maybe you need a break, Hel. Take a trip somewhere.'

'Boring! What do you think I've been doing the last six weeks?'

'Get back to work then.'

'What for?'

'Everyone's got to earn a living.'

Helena rolled her eyes.

'LOL, Webs. How much did I make last year? I lost count at, like, ten million. So I don't *have* to do anything.'

'You're free then. Think of all the twenty-two year old girls who'd give anything to be in your place. Chin up, doll-face.'

'Then why aren't I happy?' Helena wailed.

Webster gazed at his client over the top of his reading glasses. With three young daughters of his own, he was used to the odd tempest. When Helena started sniffling, he went so far as to gather his portly frame and waddle across the room to give her a kindly pat on the shoulder. When she'd calmed down, he made it back to the desk and put on a patient expression.

'Look Hel, your face is on billboards in every country in the first world. Your YouTube videos gets loads of views. You're an idol for millions of girls around the world who look up to you. Isn't that enough?'

Helena sniffed.

'All I do is look pretty and cool.'

'And?' Webster spread his arms.

'It's just, like, there's got to be more to life. Know what I mean?'

Webster sighed and took off his glasses.

'Oh dear. I always hoped this day would never come. I said to myself I just hope Hel can sail on through without the mid-life crisis. But there you go - ennui trumps ecstasy. You've had nothing but fun for years, until one day you wake up emptier than a PC joke book and ask yourself if that's all there is.'

Helena blinked back tears.

'Yeah, that's about it, Webs.'

'So you're faced with the dilemma most successful people go through at some stage. You don't need any more money or fame. Really you never have to work again. So why do you even get out of bed in the morning? It's the old existential dilemma. The burden of freedom and no idea what to do with it.'

'So what should I do?'

'That's up to you. What do you *want* to do?'

Helena gazed into the distance for a moment.

'I want to do something artistic.'

'But you *are* a work of art, doll-face, every time you step on the runway.'

'I want to make one, not be one. I want to do something talented like Taylor does.'

'Well, what then?'

'You know what? I might write a book. That'd be cool.'

'A book?' said Webster, surprised. He paused for a moment. 'Can you write?'

'I'm on Twitter all the time.'

'I mean something longer than 140 characters? Are you sure you've got it in you?'

'Like, wow, Webs - don't be a hater! You're meant to be on my team.'

'Sure, hon, I'm just trying to be practical. You know, it's not such a bad idea. What's that Heidi says? One day you're in, the next day you're out. We don't want you getting stale. A new project might be just the thing to freshen you up.'

'That's definitely what I need.'

'I suppose the actual writing isn't such a big deal. We can outsource that part. After all, Helena Bentley is a team, and there's no I in team. Who cares if it's you writing it or not?'

'I might have a try anyway.' said Helena. 'It can't be that hard.'

Webster frowned, remembering some of her tweets.

'I'm not sure that's necessary, Hel.'

Then he shrugged.

'Oh well, why not? Give it a go, and we'll get a ghostie in to tidy it up when you're done. Go for it!'

'A what?'

'A ghost writer, honey. They're professional authors who help celebs tell their stories. I mean, you could come up with some ideas, but these guys just put it in book form. It's like when makeup does you up for a shoot. They're just helping you look your best.'

'Awesome, Webs. Let's do it!'

II

Helena walked out of the office a lot happier than she'd arrived. And long story short, it wasn't long before the short story was out. Helena Bentley, author, if you don't mind. She even came up with some character names and plot ideas too during her meetings with the ghost writer, Sharon Simons. It was actually quite fun having meetings with Shaz, as Helena called her, and of course the mousy Shaz adored hanging out with the glamorous Hel as well.

Finally, the big day arrived, when Shaz came over with a beautiful advance copy of the book, *Heartbreak Heaven* by Helena Bentley. Helena's mouth fell open, then she squealed.

'O. M. G! I love it!'

Over the next two days, she read with wonder the story she'd written, and when the last page was done, jumped onto Twitter.

'So excited!! My book on shelves next week! Being an author - so cool !!!'

It really was pretty fantastic seeing her book in the shops and watching it shoot to the top of the Young Adult hit list. From there, it was a whirlwind few weeks of success, until one day she dropped into Webster's office for another chat.

'How's my little bestselling author?' he said.

'Awesome, Webs. I love being creative.'

Webster beamed at her from behind his desk.

'I've got to hand it to you, kid. I thought it was a silly idea at first, but you pulled it off. Have you thought of a new story for your next book?'

'Aw, I don't know. It's cool being an author and all - really cool - but I've kind of done that now. It's sort of ticked off my bucket list, know what I mean?'

'You can't have a bucket list at twenty-two.'

Helena rolled her eyes.

'Whatevs, Webs. Look, I've done books now. I might do some art next?'

'You mean *art* art?'

'Yeah. I loved art class at school. It was super cool.'

'I see. Well, what kind of art? Painting? Sculpture? Avant-garde?'

Helena wrinkled her pretty little nose.

'Nothing too weird. I'm more into the classics. You know, like the Moaning Lisa.'

'That's a *Simpsons* episode, hon. You mean the Mona Lisa. It's an oil painting.'

'Oil painting. That's it. That's what I want to do.'

'Have you ever painted?'

'Sort of - but let's get one of those ghost thingies in again.'

'A ghost painter? Gee, I don't know. Ghost writers, sure, but a ghost *painter*! I've never heard of such a thing.'

'Oh come on, Webs, I'm bored.'

Webster stroked his chin and looked thoughtful.

'I've got to hand it to you, babe. You're thinking outside the box. And now I come to think of it, they say Rembrandt got his apprentices to do some of the hackwork for him when he ran out of time. I suppose that's *sort* of like being a ghost painter.'

'So we can?'

'OK hon, why the hell not? I'm going to get you a ghost painter!'

Well, hot damn. Only two months later Helena Bentley had her first small painting exhibition at Shonkley's in London. She and her gal pals swanned around on opening night like they owned the place, and the pics made all the magazine covers. 'Bentley Does it Again,' one screamed. 'Is there nothing Helena Can't Do?' said the next.

Still, once again, everything gets old. Three weeks later, Helena was back in her agent's office.

'I'm bored with art,' she said. 'I feel like being sporty this time.'

'Sporty how?' said Webster.

'I want to win Wimbledon.'

Webster stared at her for a moment, trying to take this in.

'You mean playing tennis?'

Helena rolled her eyes.

'No, playing hopscotch. Of course, playing tennis.'

'Girl, you're crazy. You can't win Wimbledon just because you want to.'

'I wrote a book and I had an art exhibition. Why can't I be a world class tennis player? When I signed with your agency, you said you'd get me anything. Well - get me this.'

'Good heavens, Hel, you are really pushing it this time.'

Webster looked thoughtful for a minute, then he picked up the phone and dialled one of his support staff.

'Louise? Look up the top two hundred ranked women's tennis players in the world and see if any of them look like Helena Bentley. Let me know by tonight.'

The next day, Helena was back in the office.

'Well?' she said.

Webster pursed his lips and gave a small shake of the head.

'Can't do it, hon.'

'Why not?'

'Because you'd have to... *do it*. You know, play tennis. With people watching. You can't just parade around with the trophy after the event. People want to see the performance.'

'It's not fair,' Helena said, pouting.

'Look, I tried. A couple of the East Europeans girls looked almost close enough to consider it. But one was too short, and the other was only ranked 136 in the world. There's no way she could have won Wimbledon for you.'

'Oh hell. Why can't I have a ghost tennis player?'

'Sorry doll-face, you just can't. But listen to this: how would you like to be a fencing champion?'

'A what?'

'You know, that sword fighting sport. They wear a full head mask, so no one would even know you had a ghost fencer doing it for you.'

'Lame,' said Helena, sulking.

'It's the best I can do. If you've really got your heart set on Wimbledon, I can get you a fulltime tennis coach. How about that?'

'Hmm.' Helena mused for a moment, then stamped her foot. 'Oh, who am I fooling? I'm twenty-two. Most of those bitches have been playing since they were five.'

Webster sighed.

'Why not concentrate on what you do best? Modelling.'

'Boring! Anyhow, I *am* still doing that. I just want to achieve a few other things as well.'

Helena fixed an accusing stare on her manager.

'Listen, Webster, what do I pay you for? You're taking fifteen percent, and you're not really giving much back.'

'Helena, please. What about all those contracts?'

'Who cares? That's in the past now. Maybe it's time to move on to someone else.'

'Come on. You're just going through a bad patch.'

'I'm bored with modelling. Tell you what, Webs, you'd better start making some real changes. You've got the weekend. When I come in Monday I want to hear your ideas on what sort of ghost people you can get so I can start achieving new things.'

'Ghost people? Come on, hon. Is this a joke?'

'Don't come-on-hon me, Webster. I want a ghost squad in here by the end of next week or we're through.'

'Oh my lord. I've been in the biz a long time and thought I'd seen it all. A ghost squad!'

'That's right. I want at least six ghosts on my team, so you'd better get started. I mean, what do I pay you for?'

'OK babe, don't get angry. I'll see what I can do.'

III

The next Monday, Helena walked into the office and passed three women and three men sitting on the sofas in reception.

'There you go,' said Webster, when she'd walked inside. 'Your ghost squad. You're going to be a real polymath.'

'What's math got to do with it?' said Helena

'A polymath is someone who's good at a lot of different things. That's you now, thanks to the talented guys and gals out in the lobby. Maybe we should call them Team Polymath.'

'That sucks. Ghost squad is far cooler.'

'Whatever you say, hon. Do you want to meet them?'

'Sure. Bring them in.'

The six ghosties were called into the office, where they lined up and stood to attention.

'Welcome Ghost Squad,' said Webster. 'Step forward one at a time, then state your special skill.'

A young woman stepped forward. 'Screenwriter,' she said.

A man next to her followed. 'Inventor.'

The parade continued.

'Singer-songwriter.'

'Scientist.'

'Entrepreneur.'

When roll call was complete, Webster addressed the team.

'Welcome guys. Before we go on, did you all sign your confidentiality agreements? Yes? Splendid. You're all being handsomely paid so let's be clear that any breach of contract will cause you to forfeit any monies earned and bring on a lawsuit to boot. Right, let's get on. I'm sure you all recognise the young lady to my left.'

Helena smiled magnificently. The star-struck squad stared at her.

'Let me tell you why you're here,' Webster continued. 'As you know, Helena's a very talented model, but what you may *not* know is she has a large number of other talents as well. Art, writing, sports - you name it. Now the thing is, Helena's extremely time-poor. Between her modelling and her charity work, she simply doesn't have time to express her many talents and ambitions. That's where you guys come in. Each of you is going to liaise with Helena and myself to articulate the many talents Helena has but doesn't have time to develop.'

Everyone on the team looked thrilled. Some of them actually blushed when Helena glanced at them. Webster seemed pleased and wound up his briefing.

'I'm going to send you all to lunch, then get you in one on one to discuss the individual tasks you'll be taking on. But you all need to understand there's no I in Helena Bentley and there's no I in team. So put your egos away, you are Helena's ghost squad. It's all about squad goals not individual goals. If we all work really hard together, there's no telling what Helena might achieve.'

The squad departed to enjoy a lavish lunch and reflect on their changing fortunes. They were all talented individuals who had longed for the time and funding to work on their passions fulltime. Here, at last, was that once in a lifetime chance. Sure, Helena Bentley might take the credit, but at least they were getting well over 100K each for the chance to work on something they loved.

And it worked. Thanks to the ghost squad, Helena Bentley was able to record a pop album of original music, invent a new app, publish a scientific paper on genetics, write a screenplay, and even play a bit of tennis just for fun thanks to some ghostie coaching. It was truly amazing what Helena was able to accomplish, and all in the same year. It was so inspirational there was some loose speculation Helena might one day be up for a Nobel prize. In the meantime, however, she was honoured with an invitation from her old school to visit and give a talk to inspire the current students.

Helena accepted, glad to give something back. That she'd been a poor student herself, so must have learned everything after school, didn't reflect well on formal education - but this was overlooked. One morning just after recess, Helena addressed the assembled multitudes of aspiring young girls at her former school. Her message, although punctuated by stories of glamour trips and social events, came through loud and clear.

'Girls,' she said. 'I was once an ordinary student like you, but look how much I've achieved. It's all thanks to believing in my dreams, living them, and working hard - along with a little positive thinking. If I can do it, so can you. So here's my message to every one of you. YOU GO, GIRL!'

And with that triumphant affirmation, Helena walked offstage to a thunderous ovation. What came next, however, was a surprise. Just a few days later, Helena walked into her agent's office once again.

'Webs, I'm bored.'

'Not again? Perhaps it's time to put some new blood into the ghost squad.'

'No. That's not the answer.'

'What then?'

Helena looked thoughtful.

'When I said I was bored, that's not really right. I'm not bored. I'm interested.'

'You're speaking in riddles, hon. What do you mean?'

'I've been on a weird trip lately, ever since I became an author – and it's sort of made me think.'

Webster checked his watch, then his appointment diary. It was a slow day, so what the hell?

'OK doll-face, tell me about it.'

'That's the first thing I want to change,' said Helena. 'Stop calling me hon and doll-face and all those other names. It's sort of disrespectful, you know. I'm not a kid anymore.'

Webster raised his eyebrows a little.

'Then how about just Helena?' he said.

'Fine. That's my name. Anyhow, I've got to tell you I haven't really been happy for a while now. Yeah, it was kind of exciting doing all this creative stuff and winning awards. Then it got old.'

'You're really quite hard to please.'

'I know – and it's my own fault. I realise that now.'

Webster raised his eyebrows at that, not a little this time, but as far as they would go.

'Really, Helena? That's the first time I've heard you say anything like that.'

'I've changed, Webs. You know, it didn't hit me 'til I went back to my old school as a role model, with all the girls looking up at me like I was a superhero.'

'You've been on the runway since you were fifteen. Aren't you used to it by now?'

'That's different. I sort of deserved that. But at the school, those girls thought I was a writer, a painter, a scientist, and I felt kind of... phony. Know what I mean?'

'No comment, Hel, but do go on.'

'So all the girls are looking up at me like I'm a real heroine, and it hit me that it wasn't really me doing any of those things they thought I'd done. Of course, I knew that before, but I sort of stopped myself thinking it through, right? Like I was in denial.'

Helena sighed.

'Then after the speech was done, I went back to my hotel room and thought *what's the point*? What's the point of pretending I'm an awesome painter or a researcher or whatever? It's just me trying to be amazing, trying to get people to love and admire me. But if they're just loving a lie, what's the point?'

'How about we call your doctor, Helena? Some antidepressants might be just the ticket.'

'No, you don't understand. I'm not depressed, I'm sort of happy. Because I realised I don't need all that phony love and admiration for stuff I've never done. The thing is, I've got a whole new plan.'

'Oh yes?' Webster said doubtfully.

'The plan is I'm going to actually start doing this stuff myself, but without putting it out in public. Even if I'm no good at it, I can still do it. See, when Michael showed me how to paint, it was actually sort of cool in itself. And when Jacqui taught me the science stuff, it was kind of interesting too. Even learning tennis with Beck - I never played before, but it was really fun.'

'So you've got some new hobbies. That's good.'

'Yeah, and you know what, Webs? Who cares if I'm the best? It doesn't matter if I'm awesome at it or just average.'

'Look, Hel, this is all very well, but you're not giving up modelling are you?'

'Why should I? It's how I earn a living, and that gives me the chance to do all these other things. But I don't have to do them in public anymore.'

'You want me to disband the ghost squad?'

'No way. I'm going to keep them all on as tutors to teach me their skills.'

'Alright. If that's what you really want and as long as you keep modelling to pay for it.'

'Easy. I can pay them all a year's wages from just a couple of contracts. They can teach me and spend the rest of the time on their own work.'

Webster smiled.

'Helena. My brief has always been to keep you happy, but the way you're going, you've just about made me redundant. I just hope you keep me on for old times' sake.'

'Sure. You've been here for me in good times and bad. I'm keeping you on with the rest of the team.'

'Well, bravo the ghost squad.'

'Don't call them that. They're Team Polymath now. That's what I'm going to be.'

'Helena the polymath? I like it. You're really going to be the girl who's got it all. Beauty, wealth, and brains.'

'Beauty fades, Webs. I can't stop that, but I can do something about the rest. Now, let me take you to lunch.'

Webster raised his eyebrows once more. Then he stood up, put on his coat and scarf, linked arms with Helena, and walked out the door.

Eleven

I

Graeme Hillman had just parked his Ford when 'Heartbreak Hotel' came on the radio. Instead of pulling out the car key, he lit up a cigarette. When the Elvis classic was replaced by the Stones' 'I Can't Get No Satisfaction,' he stubbed out his smoke in the ashtray, got out of the car, and entered the offices of Dr Gideon Mackay, psychologist.

He sat in the waiting room, legs crossed, absently smoking another cigarette. These visits always made him nervous. Frankly, he had no real idea why he was here, yet somehow these sessions had become part of his routine. He considered himself a man with very few complaints in life. Yet he found himself back in this office time after time.

For his type, Hillman was average in every respect. He was a presentable, thirty-three year old, dark-haired Australian man, just under six feet tall. He was neatly dressed in trousers and a light-blue collared shirt. Only the occasional twitch of his left cheek hinted at any inner unrest.

With a complete lack of interest, he thumbed through some old copies of *Readers Digest*. He assumed Dr Mackay was busy with another patient, for he'd been waiting over ten minutes. Yet when the receptionist called him through, no one came out of the consulting room. He stood up, stubbed out his cigarette in the glass ashtray and walked through the door.

'Ah, Mr Hillman. Come in.'

In appearance, Gideon Mackay was a classic psychologist, as if he'd set out to model Freud himself. The neat, greying beard and scholarly spectacles were straight out of the textbook, as were the tidy bookshelves and soothingly bland paintings that made up the internal decor of his room. Mackay did not stand or offer a handshake. He remained seated behind his desk, flicking through a pile of papers.

'Sit down, Mr Hillman. How have you been?'

'Fine. I don't even know why I'm here. I suppose Louise has got something to do with it.'

'No doubt your wife cares for you a great deal. Are you still having the headaches? The memory losses?'

'Every now and then. Surely there's a pill for that. I don't see why I have to come here.'

Dr Mackay levelled a long, blank stare at his client, before he spoke.

'I think we're both aware that your problems aren't physical. If they were, I'd have sent you to a medical doctor.'

'You saying I'm a kook? Is that it?'

'Mental health,' said Mackay, 'is everyone's concern. It's nothing to be ashamed of. Tell me, Graeme. When your car's not working, what do you do? Take it to a mechanic. When your mind's out of alignment, you take it to a mind mechanic. You're just here for a tune up.'

'OK, Doc. If you put it like that. I suppose there *have* been a couple of weird incidents of late.'

'Oh yes?'

Hillman sat back in the chair and closed his eyes.

'It's not really an *incident*,' he said. 'Just a mood. It was a Saturday afternoon and I was playing golf. Nine holes, it was meant to be, but Browny talked me into staying on for eighteen. I was in a run of form so I agreed. But the St George game was going to be on TV. St George against Manly.'

'St George? Ah yes, your rugby obsession.'

'It's rugby *league*, not rugby. Well, I rang my wife and got her to tape the game so I could watch it when I got home.'

Hillman lapsed into silence. It went on so long the doctor offered a gentle prompt.

'Don't tell me she forgot to tape it?' he said with a smile.

'Oh no. She knows what St George means to me. She knows I'd go off my head if that happened.'

'I see,' said Mackay, raising his eyebrows a little. 'But tell me. If you're such a big fan, why didn't you go to the game?'

'All the way to Manly? I'm not crossing the bridge for them. And truth be told, there was a little... altercation last time. I reckon I'll stay away for a while.'

'Oh really?'

'But that's not the point. Point is, I got home, had a quick steak, then put the game on - and that's when it happened. See, I'm sitting there all tense, swearing at the TV, getting into it like I always do. Then suddenly it hit me - I was only watching a replay. I realised the game was already over. It had been won and lost hours ago. By now, the players were showered and dressed, probably having a steak and a beer like I was.'

'I'm not sure I understand the problem.'

'Don't you see, Doctor? All my cheering, my swearing at the TV, my excitement and fear... it was all useless. The result was already decided, so my emotions were completely futile.'

Dr Mackay adjusted his glasses and looked at his patient closely.

'Don't you think you're taking it a bit too seriously? It's not a matter of life and death. It's just a game of football.'

Hillman bristled and sat up in his chair.

'Not to me it ain't, Doc. St George is my life. Kearney, Provan, Raper, Gasnier. I live and die by those blokes. I'd lay down my life for the Red V.'

'The what?'

'The jersey. The all white with the big red V.'

Mackay said nothing for a few moments, waiting for

Hillman to calm down.

'Let's get back to your... sense of futility. You say you felt useless, watching the playback of the game.'

'Exactly. It was sort of artificial, you know, like there was no point cheering. As if the game had played out long ago, like it was all done and dusted and locked up in a museum somewhere. But that ain't the worst of it, Doc. That was only the start.'

Hillman shuddered and ran his fingers through his hair.

'The next week, St George were on TV again. The Souths game. This time I made sure I stayed home to watch it live.'

'Live on TV?'

'Yeah. So the game started and the same thing happened. I'm sweating, swearing, yelling at the TV. My wife even asked me to keep it down. That's when I realised I was trying a bit too hard.'

'What do you mean?'

'I was trying too hard to get excited, to show that I cared about the game. But the whole time I had the same feeling as the week before - that it was already over and all my cheering was useless.'

'You said it was a live broadcast, didn't you?'

'That's the point. There was something off about the whole thing. It's like the whole game was predestined to pan out a certain way no matter what I or anyone else did.'

'And what does that suggest to you?'

'That our whole lives are pointless. That everything's all mapped out and nothing we do really counts.'

Dr Mackay regarded his client sternly for a moment, then smiled.

'That wasn't quite the answer I expected. I never realised football fans could be so philosophical. Did you ever study it?'

'I've been studying football all my life.'

'Philosophy, I mean. There's a fellow named Nietzsche had a theory everything's on a permanent loop. That's what your predestination theory reminds me of. Of course, some other philosophers say there's no such thing as free will. We feel like we have it, but it's an illusion.'

'I don't know about any of that fancy stuff, Doc. I just want to get back to where I was.'

Mackay adjusted his glasses once more, and put down his pen.

'Mr Hillman, there's something I don't understand. You say that when you stayed on to play golf, your wife taped the game for you.'

'That's right.'

'How did she do that?'

Hillman frowned.

'Video, I suppose.'

'Then tell me - what year is this?'

'What sort of a ridiculous question is that?'

'It's a simple enough question. What year is it?'

Hillman stared into the distance.

'I always work it out by grand finals. We beat Manly in '59, then Easts in '60. That was our fifth premiership in a row. Then it was three against Wests, the last one in the mud. That was our eighth - in '63, the last one I remember. So - it must be 1964.'

'If you don't mind me saying, that's an awfully roundabout way to answer my question, which, as you'll agree, was a simple one. I asked you what the year is.'

'You calling me a kook?'

'I'm not calling you anything, Mr Hillman - just asking how your wife taped the game off TV in 1964.'

'I told you - with a video.'

'And what is that?'

'I... don't know. Look, who cares how it happened? It must have been a replay. Yeah, that's it. The ABC showed a replay on TV and I watched it that night when I got home.'

'You seemed very sure. You said you stayed on to play golf and called your wife asking her to tape the game for you. It's right here in my notes.'

'What does it matter? Look, Doc, I don't know what you're driving at but I've just about had enough of this.'

'I agree. That's enough for one session. But I do want you to speak to my secretary and make another appointment.'

Dr Mackay picked up his phone.

'Miss Ainscough, could you come in here a moment?'

The unusual name he pronounced as aynes-co. Almost at once, the door opened and a tall blonde woman entered the room.

'Book Mr Hillman another session,' said Mackay.

Hillman stood up abruptly.

'Don't bother, Doc. I'm done with this.'

'It's too late, Graeme. We have to go through with it now. Miss Ainscough?'

The secretary approached Hillman and slapped him hard across the face. He immediately put his hand to his cheek.

'What the hell did you do that for?' he cried. 'You've ruined everything!'

He turned and ran for the door, but tripped and found himself sprawled on the floor. He turned his head and saw Mackay and Ainscough looking down at him.

II

'Ah, Mr Hillman. Nice to see you again. How are the headaches?'

'They come and they go,' said Hillman. 'It don't bother me.'

He was back in Dr Mackay's office again. He looked around at the white walls, neat bookcases, and soothingly bland paintings. There was a framed certificate on the wall licensing Gideon Mackay to practice psychology.

'You're feeling better then?' Mackay said.

'Have we met before? You look familiar.'

'Mr Hillman, you've been coming to my office every year since 1956.'

'Ah '56. The start of our golden run. The greatest sporting achievement our country's ever seen.'

'I must say the Melbourne Olympics brought a tear to my eye too.'

'Not the Olympics. St George. Eleven premierships in a row and it all started in '56 with the win over Balmain.'

'Oh, I see.'

'It's God's own football team. Provan, Raper, Gasnier, Langlands. We've never seen their like before and we won't again.'

'I see you haven't forgotten your football obsession. But eleven in a row, you say, starting in 1956. It's '65 now so that must be nine.'

'I stand corrected, Doctor. Nine in a row, and long may they reign, the mighty Dragons.'

Dr Mackay made a note in his notebook.

'Last time you spoke about your sense of despondency. Your feeling that everything's predestined and all your actions are futile. Do you still feel that way?'

'Well, Doc, that's probably how all the mugs who don't follow St George feel. Just imagine what it's like kicking off another season against the might of Gasnier, Langlands, and co! Year after year they line up for another beating - Wests, Manly, Newtown, Balmain. As for Norths and Canterbury, I don't think they've got a win over us in the last ten years.

Even Souths have slunk away in shame and despair - how the mighty have fallen!'

'Why are you so obsessed with football?'

'I'm not. I'm obsessed with St George.'

'Why?'

'Because we are the best. Ryan, Kearney, Walsh - what a side! Even Poppa Clay had a stint in reserves, that's how good we are. And him with eight grand finals to his name. That's why St George always wins.'

'Do they, Mr Hillman?'

'We might drop the odd game through the season, but we always win when it counts - the grand final. We always win that.'

'Doesn't it get boring to win all the time?'

'Never. It's only right that we win. We are St George.'

'I must say I admire your passion, single-minded though it is. I don't quite understand it, but I admire it.'

'Which team do you follow, Dr Mackay? Don't tell me you're a Norths fan. If so, we'd better swap chairs!'

'I don't follow rugby, Mr Hillman, I'm from Melbourne. I support Collingwood in the VFL.'

Hillman winced.

'Never could make head nor tail of that sport. Aerial ping pong! Collingwood, you say. Are they any good?'

'I don't mean to brag, but we did win four titles in a row back in the twenties.'

Hillman stifled a laugh.

'Four in a row! Well, well. I suppose not everyone can win eleven in a row like St George. Four's not bad, really. We achieved that back in '59, then kept going. Four in a row. It's something you Melbourne people can be proud of.'

'You never know. One day Melbourne might have their own rugby team competing against your beloved St George.'

Hillman laughed loudly.

'Melbourne playing rugby league? They'll put a man on the moon before that happens!'

'You seem very sure.'

'It's ridiculous, Doc. Laughable!'

'Why are you getting upset over such a trivial remark?'

'Because it's rubbish, Doctor Mackay. You're supposed to be curing my headaches yet you insult my intelligence with an absurdity like that. I've had just about enough of this. I'm out of here.'

Hillman stood up and walked towards the door. Mackay picked up his phone.

'Miss Ainscough?'

The receptionist appeared at the door.

'Get away from me,' said Hillman.

She slapped him hard across the face. He recoiled.

'Ow! What the hell did you do that for? You've ruined everything.'

III

'Ah, Mr Hillman, come in. Sit down.'

'Thanks. Doctor... ?'

'Mackay. Doctor Mackay. Still troubled by the memory lapses, I see.'

'They come and go.'

'Like the headaches, then.'

'I don't let it worry me, Doc.'

'Let's start with the basics, shall we? Just answer a few simple questions.'

Dr Mackay picked up a pen and his notebook.

'Name?'

'Graeme Hillman.'

'Address?'

'44 Barnaby road, Hurstville.'

'Age?'

'Thirty-three.'

'Date of birth?'

'May 22nd, 19... what year is it now?'

'You tell me, Mr Hillman.'

'I always work it out by the grand finals. Easts in '60. That was our fifth. Three against Wests, the last in the mud in '63. Then there was Balmain in '64, and last year Souths with the record crowd. Must have been '65. Ten premierships in a row - that's unheard of! And that means it's 1966. So using my elementary powers of subtraction I guess I was born in 1933. Quite a coincidence eh, Doc. Born in '33, and I'm 33.'

'Why are you so obsessed with St George?'

'I'm not obsessed, I just like to celebrate greatness - and we are the best. Provan, Kearney, Langlands, Clay...'

'Gasnier, Raper, Mundine,' finished Dr Mackay.

'Never heard of that last one, Doc. Must be one of your Collingwood boys.'

'Five-eighth, wasn't he?'

'You're mistaken there. Raper played five-eighth in the '62 grand final, Pollard in '63. Apart from that, it was Brian 'Poppa' Clay all the way.'

'You know that's not true. Why don't you stop pretending?' Hillman stood up.

'Look at you. A Melbourne boy trying to tell me about the mighty St George! I'll not stand for this, Doctor.'

'I believe you just did, Mr Hillman. Now, if you don't sit down again, I'm going to have to call my secretary.'

Hillman made a dash for the exit but tripped and found himself sprawled on the floor inches from the door.

'Missed it by that much,' said Mackay. 'Go and sit down.'

Hillman shuffled back to his chair. Mackay regarded him sternly.

'Why is St George so important to you? It's just a football team, not a matter of life and death.'

'Yes it is. This ain't football, it's war!'

'Mr Hillman, please. You say you were born in 1933. That means you lived through a real war. Your father probably served in it, right? A little perspective, perhaps.'

'Don't tell me about the war, Doc. My father never came back.'

'I'm sorry to hear that. Would you like to talk about it?'

'It was a long time ago. I'd sooner forget it. But who needs a father when you've got St George? There's thirteen fathers every time they walk onto Kogarah Oval.'

'And your wife? What does she think of your obsession?'

'She puts up with it. Doesn't understand it, but she puts up with it. Sometimes if I'm watching a big game on TV, I actually make her leave the house. She goes to her sister's for the night.'

'I see.'

'Otherwise there's no telling what I might do. I've been known to break things, throw stuff at the wall. I just get so involved in the game, know what I mean? My wife says I ought to show that much passion in the bedroom!'

'But Mr Hillman, I thought you said you had a sense of futility watching the game, like the result was predestined.'

He picked up his notebook.

'... as if the action had all played out long before. It was all done and dusted and locked up in a museum somewhere. That's what you said.'

'I don't recall that, Doctor.'

'I can't help you if you lie, Mr Hillman. Answer me this: why does St George always have to win?'

'Because we are the best!' yelled Hillman. 'We always win. Provan, Porter, Langlands...'

'Blacklock, Barrett, McGregor,' shouted Dr Mackay.

'We won eleven titles in a row,' said Hillman. 'No one can ever take them off us.'

'You said it was ten.'

Hillman leapt to his feet.

'I never did.'

'Ten! You said ten, soon as you came in.'

'Ten, eleven, twelve, fifteen. We'll win a hundred, because we are St George and we'll go on forever!'

'Sit down, Mr Hillman, or I'm going to have to sedate you.'

There was a standoff. Dr Mackay stared into Hillman's eyes for a long moment, until Hillman at last looked away and sat down. He buried his face in his hands.

There was a long silence. At last, Mackay spoke, in calm, measured tones.

'Mr Hillman. This has gone on long enough. Now, I put it to you that your memory losses, your headaches, leave you in a state of continual anxiety, which in turn leaves you desperate to cling to the one thing that feels certain - the supremacy of St George in rugby league. I also put it to you that the entire concept is an illusion, and that only by letting go of this false idea can you free yourself from your own enslavement. St George doesn't always win.'

'They do. It's a historical fact. Look it up. Eleven in a row.'

'They don't. You know it. I know it. We all know it.'

'We always win. We are St George. So it is and will always be.'

'I put it to you further, Mr Hillman, that you were not born in 1933.'

'I never said I was sure. I just counted back from our premierships.'

'You never saw any of those premierships. You were born in 1966.'

'I saw 'em all, goddamn you!'

'You were a babe in arms when they won their last.'

'You're crazy. I'm not listening to this rubbish.'

'You might not listen to me, Mr Hillman, but here's someone else to tell it to you.'

The office door opened. Hillman looked up and saw a granite-jawed, rock-hard man. He looked like an old school cop, tough enough to put the wind up the hardest crim of 1960s Sydney.

'Kevin Ryan?' said Hillman in disbelief.

'Morning, Graeme,' said Ryan, extending his hand to shake.

Hillman felt his hand engulfed in the giant paw of the great St George forward.

'An honour to meet you, Mr Ryan - but what are you doing here?'

'I've come to give you the truth. Then I'm going to take you away.'

'What for? I've done nothing wrong.'

'Don't make me hurt you, son.'

'I don't want any trouble with you, Mr Ryan. Not with the hardest forward who ever took the field for St George.'

'Not me. That was Billy Wilson. Kearney, Provan, Rasmussen... no one soft ever played for St George.'

'Wait. I remember now. I remember what you did.'

'Let's go. Your time is up.'

'Why should I go with you? It's your fault we lost. You went to Canterbury in '67.'

'All things come to an end.'

'Eleven in a row, then you went to Canterbury and helped them knock us out in the final. You're a traitor! We could have had twelve, thirteen, a hundred!'

'That's football, son. Nothing lasts forever. Now, I'm warning you. Either come quietly or I'll take you out myself.'

'You betrayed us. All of us who sat on the hill at Kogarah and the SCG. You let down your mates. Langlands, Walsh, and Johnny King. What about Huddart and Maddison? They only got one title thanks to you. They could have had another three or four if you hadn't left us. What the hell did you do that for? You've ruined everything.'

Ryan looked sideways at Dr Mackay, then turned and punched Hillman hard on the jaw. Hillman blacked out. By the time he woke up again, the psychologist's office had gone and he was sitting in a darkened theatre watching a scene unfold.

IV

September 26th, 1999. Grand final day. The great St George rugby league club had merged with another team, Illawarra, to become St George-Illawarra. Graeme Hillman, like many other fans, chose to ignore this. They were the St George Dragons and always would be. Today, in the grand final, they were up against another newly formed club, the Melbourne Storm.

He'd thought about going to the game but ruled it out. Crowds, transport, long queues for a beer, and no TV commentary. Better to stay home and watch it on TV in his comfortable lounge room at 44 Barnaby road, Hurstville.

Louise had been given strict instructions. She was to be out of the house by noon and not return for twenty-four hours. It was a rule applied whenever St George had a grand final, or a big semi final. Used to this by now, she'd arranged to stay with her sister.

'Nothing personal,' Hillman said. 'But you know me. As soon as the game kicks off, the atmosphere's going to get pretty volatile round here. Better stay outside a one mile radius.'

'You're a pain, Graeme,' his wife replied. She was a petite brunette of Italian descent. After seven years of marriage, she accepted her husband's odd obsession, but went through the ritual of complaining just to hold her end up.

'It probably won't matter,' said Hillman. 'I mean, it's only the Storm. A rugby league team from Melbourne. Have you ever heard of anything so ridiculous? But stay away, just in case it gets close - and don't come back tonight. I'll probably be that drunk after the game you wouldn't want to come near me anyway.'

Louise glowered.

'Just make sure you don't break anything this time. If I find even one mark on the wall, you'll be repainting. Got it?'

'Come on, Lou. I ain't broke anything since the '96 grand final. Ridge was tackled and they let him play on to set up a try. What do you expect me to do? It was only the turning point of the game!'

'I don't care, Graeme. Losing a game of football's not worth smashing up your house for.'

'I'll do anything for the Red V. I'll smash up my own house and the neighbour's as well, if it comes to it.'

'Calm down. It's only ten to twelve and you're already acting like a lunatic.'

'Don't say ten to twelve - it sounds like a losing score! Say twelve to ten for Christ's sake. A bit of sensitivity please.'

'I thought you said it was in the bag. You think St George will only get up by two points?'

'We smashed them 34-10 a couple of weeks ago. We'll probably win by forty this time.'

'Then stop acting so nervous.'

'Lou, no offence, but will you just go? You're meant to be out of here by twelve.'

'You're a pain, Graeme.'

'You already said that. I'm going out to buy beer. When I come back, make sure you're gone.'

'Maybe I won't come back.'

'Better bloody not - until tomorrow anyway.'

'How about a goodbye kiss?'

'No sex before the game. Oh alright, just a kiss.'

'Right. I'm off. Good luck.'

Graeme Hillman got into his car holding a small bag, inside which was ten-thousand dollars cash. He'd made several withdrawals over the last couple of weeks, ready for this day. He drove to the TAB and put it all on St George. At $1.50 for the win, it would net him a neat five-thousand dollar profit. He placed the betting receipt in his wallet, then bought a carton of beer and a bottle of Scotch.

He drove home and tried to kill time until 3pm. It was useless, but at least he could have a couple of beers to take the edge off. He suffered through the preliminaries, the build up, and the national anthem, until at last the game finally kicked off and the terror began.

Much as he tried, Hillman could not sit still upon the couch he'd placed at optimum viewing distance from the TV. After five minutes, he gave up and stood upright, shifting his weight from foot to foot every so often, clenching and unclenching his fists.

When Fitzgibbon scored for St George in the fourteenth minute, Hillman punched the air and ran around the living room with a cry of triumph. But that was nothing to what happened at the thirty minute mark when Nathan Blacklock gathered a kick and ran seventy metres to score under the posts. 14-0!

'This is ours!' Graeme Hillman shouted, opening a bottle of beer and drinking it in one swallow. At halftime, he smoked two cigarettes, basking in St George's clear ascendancy.

Melbourne got a penalty goal just after halftime to make it 14-2. Then, at the fifty minute mark, St George were set to seal the win when Mundine chipped ahead and regathered - but he dropped the ball over the try line. That would have been the game. Hillman swore savagely and threw a plastic water bottle against the wall, where it left a clear chip in the paint. Looked like he'd be repainting.

That was the start of the Melbourne comeback. In an extraordinary eight minute period, they scored two tries to St George's one. With ten minutes to go, Melbourne had clawed their way back to 18-14, just four points behind. Graeme Hillman swore and sweated through the terror, feeling each blow like a mortal wound. One more score and Melbourne could steal the game.

The wave of fear built to a crescendo just before fulltime when the Melbourne half, Kimmorley, put through a high kick which was caught over the try line by his team mate, Craig Smith, who was then knocked out by a tackle from St George winger, Jamie Ainscough.

'He dropped it!' shouted Hillman. 'He dropped the ball. We've won!'

But something was very wrong and he knew it.

'Oh no. St George could be in trouble here,' said one of the TV commentators. 'Ainscough's hit him right in the head. Harrigan's sent it straight upstairs to the video ref. This could be a penalty try.'

'No. No,' said Hillman, with a howl of anguish. The St George winger, Jamie Ainscough appeared on the TV screen, hands on hips.

'What the hell did you do that for?' Hillman screamed.

'You've ruined everything!'

'He would have scored for sure,' the commentator said. 'This could be a penalty try. That means they'll kick the conversion from right in front of the posts. This is going to give Melbourne the game.'

'No! No way!'

On the TV screen the Melbourne captain, Glenn Lazarus, could be seen walking away from the referee, Bill Harrigan, a look of disbelieving glee on his face.

'That's got to be a penalty try,' the commentator said. 'Ainscough's slapped him right in the head and knocked him out. That's a penalty try, no doubt.'

The head commentator, Ray Warren, chimed in. 'I think you'll find that Bill Harrigan is about to make one of the biggest calls ever been made in one hundred years of rugby league.'

Slowly, Graeme Hillman backed away from the TV screen. Step by agonised step, he reversed until his back was against the rear wall of the living room. Even from that distance, he could see the on-ground scoreboard about to flash up the decision. Graeme Hillman looked on in horrified refusal, a white-hot surge of fury forming inside him. Then, as he knew it would, the result flashed up on the screen. TRY.

When those three letters T-R-Y appeared on the screen, something inside him snapped. With a violent oath, he launched himself in a full pelt charge towards the TV, lowered his head like a wounded bull, and butted the screen with the full force of his rage. In so doing, he knocked himself even more senseless than the Melbourne player who'd scored the winning try.

At least he didn't have to witness the fulltime siren and the despair of the St George players and their fans.

V

'Ah, Mr Hillman. You're back.'

Hillman looked around him at the neat consulting office. There was the framed certificate on the wall licensing Gideon Mackay to practice psychology.

'How are you feeling today?' Mackay said. 'Headaches still bothering you?'

'They come and they go. I don't let it worry me.'

'I believe you've said that before.'

'Sure thing, Doc. I've got déjà vu all over again. And you won't believe the crazy dreams these headaches are giving me.'

'Oh yes?'

'I dreamt I was in the future. St George were called St George-Illawarra, and they played Melbourne in the grand final. Can you believe that? Insane! St George were up 14-0 at halftime, then one of the players dropped the ball inches from the try line, and another one gave away a penalty try in the last minute. It's your classic nightmare! Then I charged head-first into the TV and that woke me up, thank God.'

Dr Mackay sighed. He took off his glasses and placed them on the desk.

'You're still in denial. I thought surely this time we'd get through to you.'

'What are you talking about? I reckon I'm about cured now. It's probably time I got home to the wife. Must have missed a couple of St George games by now. We're not far off winning our eleventh title. Eleven in a row. Can you believe that?'

'It wasn't a dream, Mr Hillman.'

'It certainly was - and a most horrible nightmare, too. The sooner I forget it, the better.'

'It wasn't the future.'

'I agree. I mean, St George and Melbourne playing out a

grand final. When it comes to the future, I'll cop flying cars like in *The Jetsons*, but I won't cop that.'

'You need to face up to what you did. Your mind has been in denial - of St George's loss in the 1999 grand final, and what you did afterwards. You've been in Purgatory ever since - for the last eleven years.'

'What are you talking about, Doc? I thought you were a man of science.'

'So strong was your denial that you hallucinated an entire fantasy life for yourself, set during St George's eleven year reign in the fifties and sixties. You returned to a lost, halcyon age when St George were invincible.'

'They were simpler and better times. I'm glad I was born to live through that era.'

'You never lived through it. You were born in 1966. You were thirty-three when you died during the 1999 grand final.'

'It ain't fair, Doc! I always heard about the golden era but I never got to taste it.'

'Your era had its own glory.'

'The grand final win over Parramatta in '77 when I was eleven. What is it about that number? It's haunting me.'

'Was that all?'

'Sure, we beat the Bulldogs in '79, but I was just a kid. Two titles, Doc, and that's all she wrote. From '77 then eleven times two - twenty-two years later and it's 1999. We were due. It was our destiny to win it that day. Why'd you think I put on that ten-thousand bucks? I'm not normally a betting man but we couldn't lose.'

'Yet you did - and you lost far more than money. Until you accept what happened, you can't move on.'

'We can't have lost. It's a lie. A horrible nightmare. Thank God I'm back in my real life and the glory of St George. Gasnier, Smith, Walsh, Lumsden...'

Dr Mackay picked up his phone.

'Miss Ainscough. I can't get through to this fellow. We'll have to pull out the big gun. Send him in.'

The door opened and a giant of a man filled the doorway. Hillman looked up, then froze in shock.

'Mr Provan. What are you doing here?'

The square-jawed colossus walked forward and shook Hillman's hand. Hillman turned to Mackay.

'You see, Doc. The man himself. Norm Provan, St George's greatest ever captain. He don't look a day over thirty. You still want to tell me it's not 1965?'

'That's not Norm Provan. The 'man himself,' as you call him, is still alive back on Earth. One of my colleagues has agreed to take on this form in a last ditch effort to reach you.'

'That's gibberish. This is the great Norm Provan or I'm not here.'

'If you believe that, it'll help us achieve the task of waking you.'

Mackay and Provan looked at each other, as if exchanging a silent signal. Then Provan turned back to Hillman.

'Time to go home, Graeme.'

The psychologist's office vanished. Hillman found himself standing at the front door of 44 Barnaby road, Hurstville.

'Got your keys?' said Provan.'

Hillman unlocked the door and they walked into the house. They could hear the TV blaring from the living room. When they entered, Hillman caught sight of his own body, passed out in front of the TV. He was lying on his back, his head lolling slightly to the right. A small amount of blood had congealed on the top of his head and on the cream-coloured carpet, the red and the white combining in the colours of St George.

'What's this, Mr Provan? We're back in the dream.'

Hillman glanced at the wall clock, showing 12.30pm. At

that moment, there was the sound of a key in the lock, then footsteps and his wife's voice. There was a note of apprehension in it.

'Graeme, are you there?'

His wife entered the room and caught sight of his body on the floor. She ran forward and tried to rouse him, then turned off the TV and called an ambulance.

Suddenly they were in a hospital ward. Hillman looked down at his own body, hooked up to life support. He walked around the bed, examining his body from every angle, realisation dawning.

'So it's true, Mr Provan.'

'I'm sorry, Graeme. You've got to face up to what happened.'

'Did we really lose the '99 grand final to Melbourne?'

'That's right.'

'It's not fair. We were up 14-0 at halftime. They only scored in the last minute to take it off us.'

'The second half is as important as the first half, and the last minute is as important as the first. We should have beat Melbourne but we didn't. That's football, son. You can't change the past. You can only move forward.'

'I just hate losing.'

'So do I, but in sport there's always a winner and a loser. That's why we play so hard. There's no quarter asked and none given. If we win, we shake the opposition's hand with good grace, and if we lose we do the same.'

'Why'd Mundine have to drop that ball over the try line?'

'Look how many tries he scored for us that year. We wouldn't have made the grand final without him.'

'Why did Ainscough have to knock that bloke out? If he'd just let him score out wide they might have missed the kick and we would have gone to extra time.'

'That's hindsight. He was trying to stop them scoring.

Would you have done any better? We all make mistakes. Don't we?'

He nodded at Hillman's body, hooked up to the life support.

'If you'd let your wife stay home that day, maybe she could have got you to the hospital in time. You always took it too seriously. It's football. It's not life and death. Except for you, it actually was.'

'Can I go back and change it?'

'Sorry, son. The fulltime whistle has blown.'

He saw his wife walk into the room with a doctor. She held hands with the unconscious body as the doctor turned off the life support. Hillman felt a dawning terror.

'What have I done?'

'You cared too much. There are worse sins.'

'I wish I'd cared more about my wife than St George!'

'It's done and dusted now. You have to shake hands with your life. Own your mistakes and move on. Forgive yourself. There's no one living or dead never made a mistake.'

The giant figure of Norm Provan turned to him with a kindly expression.

'Let's give this story a happy ending.'

Hillman turned to him in hope.

'You'll let me go back? Give me another chance?'

'Not back. Forward. We'll go forward in time another eleven years. October 3rd, 2010. The 2010 grand final where St George have finally made it back to the big stage. Do you want to watch the game?'

'Who do we play?'

'Easts.'

'The Roosters, eh. We beat them in 1960. Not in '75 though. The towelled us up 38-0. Langlands' last big game. No, I can't stand to watch it. Just tell me the result.'

'Are you sure you want to know?'

'Yes, Mr Provan. Give it to me straight. Do we win?'

'Sure, son. We win 32-8. Gasnier's nephew Mark scores the first try.'

'Oh, thank God. At last.'

'If you don't want to watch that one, why don't we go back to '66? We can watch our grand final win against Balmain. The last in our eleven year run. Funny coincidence. We beat 'em in 56 as well to kick it all off.'

'Can we do that?'

'Let's go.'

They travelled back to the SCG in 1966 and saw St George beat Balmain 23-4, with tries to Huddart, Pollard, and Ryan. The end of St George's eleven year reign, the likes of which would never be seen again.

Nearby, in a modest suburban home in southern Sydney, a three month old Graeme Hillman kicked and gurgled in his cot.

VI

'Last stop, Graeme,' said Norm Provan. 'Time to say goodbye.'

'Where are we? When are we?'

'Rookwood cemetery. October 4th, 2010.'

Louise Parker, formerly Louise Hillman, walked into the graveyard, eleven years after Graeme had last seen her. She carried a wreath of red and white flowers. Although remarried, she never forgot her former husband. She laid the wreath upon his grave.

> Graeme Hillman
> 1966-1999
> Fondly loved and remembered

She stood in silence for a few minutes, dabbing at her eyes. Then, at last, she turned on her heel and walked away.

'Louise. Wait! I'm sorry.' Graeme called after her.

Norm Provan laid a hand on his shoulder.

'She can't hear you, son. Come on. There's a time and season for all things, and this one's done. It's time to rest and recharge, then you'll come back fresh and start again.'

The two men shook hands, there was a flash of light, and the graveyard was empty once more.

AUTHOR'S NOTE

St George's run of eleven successive titles has never been matched. They reigned from 1956-66. They won the title again eleven years later in 1977, then in 1979. The club went on to lose grand finals in 1985, 92, 93, 96, and most famously, 1999 with the last minute loss to Melbourne. St George fans had to wait another eleven long years to play a grand final, which they won in 2010 against Eastern Suburbs. St George have yet to win another title.

They're due in 2021.

Further Note - With due respect, the famous St George players Norm Provan and Kevin Ryan who appear in this story are, of course, not the actual people, but simply hallucinatory forms taken by Dr Mackay's colleagues as a way to communicate with Graeme Hillman.

At the time of writing, January 2018, both of these esteemed gentlemen are still alive in the real world.

Indian Summer

I

No matter how good the relationship, something always went wrong - and something different every time. With Rebecca it had been political views. With Gina it was money troubles. With Serena it was a farcical fight over music. Whatever girl Dave Laurence partnered with, he couldn't make it work.

On top of that, he could never get past four years. The record had been set way back in Dave's early twenties. In the three decades since, he'd never been able to break it. Take Sarah, his latest failure. They'd even gotten engaged and he was sure he'd finally beat the four year mark, just as runners once cracked the four minute mile. But wouldn't you know it? After three years and eleven months, she said she didn't want to get married after all.

'But why?' he asked for the tenth time that day, after she gave him the news.

'I want a house in the country.'

'What's wrong with our apartment? We're one block from the beach.'

'I never go.'

'People save up all year just to come here for their holidays.'

'I want a backyard and a dog.'

'What's wrong with Izzy?'

'He's alright for a cat but he's no Cocker Spaniel.'

'Can I keep him then?'

'No. Izzy's mine.'

This was true. Having brought him to the relationship, the cat was technically hers, but Dave's heart sank as he watched the little fellow being put in his carry cage and taken away when Sarah moved out the next day. That first night alone in the empty flat, he had to go out for a drink just to escape the silence.

'Why didn't you go with her?' asked his friend Ray.

'She didn't want me to. Besides, there's work. Eighteen years in the same department. You think I can just walk away? How am I going to get a public service job in the country?'

'Do something else.'

'Bit late for a career change. Anyway, we were going to get married. I would *never* have left her. Loyalty has to work both ways.'

'You'll meet someone else.'

Dave sipped his beer forlornly.

'I'm not sure I can face another trek up the mountain.'

As he struggled out of bed the next day, he realised it was true. He'd invested all his hope in Sarah - where to from here? Throw in the towel on relationships? Let the rest of his life fizzle out as a single man? Or, to give it an empowered spin, turn MGTOW, like some of the younger guys were doing these days? That is, Men Going Their Own Way, rejecting women altogether.

Well, he *could* do that, except for the practical problems. With a dawning horror, he realised he'd have to re-enter the hell of flat-sharing. Not, at least, moving into someone else's place - out of the question - but someone would have to move in with him. He'd then have to go through the routine of forming a benevolent dictatorship while pretending flat-sharing at the age of fifty-two was just what he'd always wanted.

There was no real alternative. His salary as a lowish middle manager at the Department of Transport would not stretch to cover Sydney's exorbitant rents. Even if he could take on the emotional challenge of living alone, it was too much financially. So, flat-sharing again - a ghastly prospect! Surely there was another way. Perhaps he should get a new girlfriend immediately and invite her to move in, on the off chance it might work out. It was a reckless idea and bound to end badly, but he was crazy enough to consider it.

What about Ryanna from work? She'd given clear signs of interest last year. Had he been an adulterous man he could have responded, but he'd played a dead bat to her overtures. With a sense of unease, he realised he was now free to pursue her. Still, what folly it would be. The woman - girl - was thirty at best, two decades younger than himself. They might hit it off for a while but it was only a matter of time before something went wrong.

By long habit, he forced himself into the cold shower to rouse himself from the already-tired state in which he woke more and more often these days. As he dried himself, he turned over his options once more. While he was shaving, the answer appeared.

The idea hit him with clarity, much as it must come to aging, once-elite sportsmen who realise their time is up. *Why even go on at all?* The world he'd known and loved was gone. Take music, for example. It was all streaming and playlists now, rather than the vinyl LPs he'd grown up with or the CDs he'd enjoyed in his prime. What's more, most of the bands he liked were either finished or on their last legs. He'd always been into heavy rock but all the classic bands were just about done. Sabbath had retired. Malcolm Young, AC/DC's driving force, had died only last month. Priest were about to bow out, and even Slayer had just announced a farewell world tour.

Then there were the sporting teams. He'd loved Australian cricket, but the two golden eras of his lifetime - the seventies and the nineties - were *long* past. What's worse, test cricket was dying, or so some people said. It was all T20 now - cricket for the smart-phone generation.

I'm old, he thought as he sat down at his desk. *I'm yesterday's man*. With a shock, he saw the truth of it. He began to speak the words out loud as if to understand them better. 'I'm at the point where suicide is no longer the irrational option.'

Curtain then? Maybe it really was time to 'bow out,' so to speak, and sadly no one was going to call him back for an encore. His exit wouldn't leave much of a hole in the world. His few remaining relatives would be saddened but hardly devastated. He'd lost touch with the friends of his youth, and gotten absorbed in 'couple life' at the expense of more recent friendship. Who would even miss him?

'Jesus Christ,' he said. 'It's true.'

But how to do it? Ah, the gruesome logistics. Not knives - he hated blood and blades. Not guns - too violent, and horrible for the person who found him to clean up. Besides, he'd never fired a gun in his life. A bridge jump? He couldn't stand heights. Hanging? Too macabre. It would probably have to be some kind of poison or OD. Then again, what if poison was *worse* than the alternatives? It might be slower and more painful. Didn't that nut job Jim Jones shoot himself rather than take the poison at Jonestown?

This would require some thought. Oh well, no rush. He would sort it out in due course. It was a cold Saturday morning so he put on his coat and set off for the park to think it over. He bought a coffee to drink as he walked along. A few minutes later, he looked around for a bin to throw away the empty cup, but the only one he could see was on the other side of the road some thirty metres behind him. He crossed over and tossed in the cup and was about to resume his journey when he caught sight of the veterinary clinic, where three small kittens were playing in the front window.

He leaned up against the glass and watched them. They

could not have been more than a couple of months old. One was asleep on a cushion and two more were having a play fight. The one that caught his eye was a little ginger kitten with green eyes. When it saw him looking, it walked right up to the glass and stared. How he longed to pick it up, perhaps even take it home. And at that moment Dave thought, *why not?* He saw a new path open up. Rather than going MGTOW, or topping himself, perhaps another cultural model would serve him better. Become a 'cat lady'? Maybe it would do. He wouldn't need a girlfriend any more, just a cat - and unlike the girl, the cat would never leave.

He looked again at the ginger kitten, staring up at him with hope and curiosity, and decided to take it home. Yet he immediately knew it was a selfish desire. He still had to face the problems of the morning, the very ones which had prompted thoughts of a drastic exit. The flipside of rejection was commitment. Dave knew that if he took the kitten home and loved it, he could not later abandon it if his own problems proved too much. What if it all became too hard in a couple of years? How then could he kill himself and abandon this innocent creature? After all, how long does a cat live: ten, twelve years? That was a long time for his own escape route to be closed.

He looked again at the ginger kitten, gazing up at him with those big green eyes, then turned and walked in through the vet's front door. There was a young girl at the reception desk. They all seemed young to him now. She smiled, as if pleased to see him.

'Hi. How's Ozzy?'

'Oh, you mean Izzy,' said Dave. Now he remembered the girl, and her name - Kate. He'd seen her a couple of times when he and Sarah brought Izzy in for treatment.

'No idea,' he said. 'My ex took him when she moved out.'

'Sorry to hear,' Kate replied, with a sympathetic look.

'That's why I came in,' said Dave. 'The kittens in your window - are they for adoption?'

'Sure - and we'll throw in micro-chipping and de-sexing for free.'

'Really?'

'As long as they go to good homes we don't mind.'

He stared into the distance.

'But they're kittens. How long does a cat live?'

The girl beamed.

'Ten years, at least. Fifteen. My auntie's cat went to twenty-one!'

Dave frowned and spoke quietly, as if to himself.

'So long... I can't be sure. Ten years.'

Turning back to Kate, he said, 'Do you have anyone older?'

'Older?'

'Any mature cats. You know, that have been around a bit.'

'There's Gwyn,' she replied. 'We've normally got two or three wanting re-homing, but there's just Gwyn at the moment.'

'Funny name. How'd you spell it?'

'G-W-Y-N. It's Welsh, I think.'

'What's he like? Is it a he?'

'Yeah - a beautiful old tabby, twelve years old. Loves people, loves attention. Want to meet him?'

She led Dave off to a room at the back of the clinic, and there was Gwyn. An old grey cat, dozing in an enclosure. He half opened an eye when they approached, then shut it again.

'Skinny old boy, isn't he?' Dave remarked.

'That's not unusual for an older cat,' said Kate. 'Let's take him out.'

She reached into the enclosure and picked up the cat, then handed him over. Gwyn began purring at once.

'I think he's chosen you,' said Kate.

Gwyn's fur was very soft, like a rabbit's. Dave stroked it, and felt the cat's slender bulk. He didn't weigh much more than a big bottle of milk. Dave remembered his mood of the morning, his dark urges. They seemed to have receded, just like a bad dream.

'Twelve years old?' he said aloud. 'That's not bad. Not bad at all.'

'He could go another five at least,' said Kate brightly. 'With the right love and care.'

'Five!'

She misinterpreted Dave's look of concern.

'Or ten. You never know.'

'Ten?' he repeated. 'Oh my god. Then again, it might just be one or two.'

'Who knows?' said Kate.

Dave made up his mind.

'I'll risk it. And however long it is, so be it. When he goes, I go.'

The words made no sense to Kate, so she simply turned to walk back to the desk.

'I'll get the paperwork.'

II

Gwyn settled into his new home like he was born there. Not just into Dave's flat, but the whole address. The cat became a familiar sight at the block of units, sitting sociably on the stairs watching the flow of people into the various apartments. Most of them would stop to give him a pat or a scratch under the chin. He'd even go into the apartment below Dave's for a change of scene. Although he was on 'frenemy' status with the cat therein, its human owner enjoyed his visits.

It was surprising what a difference the cat made. Dave no longer found himself fretting over the departed Sarah. An amiable creature, Gwyn sat beside him on the sofa, or slept on the desk while he was using the computer. In Dave's mind, the idea of a future began to open out. His job wasn't that bad, really. Sharing the flat wouldn't be so terrible either. He'd done it before, he could do it again - and indeed, three weeks after Gwyn's arrival, a polite mature-aged university student moved into the spare room. Between studying and a part time job, the guy wasn't around enough to be any real bother.

As for the cat, he did have a few annoying habits - like demanding food at 4am, or jumping onto the rim of the bathtub and meowing for the tap to be turned on. The running water was apparently so much better than the water in his bowl. Its other peculiarity was the 'bedtime song.' For some reason, when Dave went to bed at night, the cat saw fit to perform an odd series of meows and squeaks as it settled down on the doona beside him. Perhaps its mother had taught it to him in the kitten crew all those years ago. After lights went out, however, Gwyn had the awkward habit of creeping up to the pillow beside Dave's head right next to his face. At a loss how to respond to this flattering show of affection, Dave tried to put up with it for a few minutes, then he'd give up and turn his body around so the cat was behind him. At this point, Gwyn would very patiently and politely stand up, walk a semicircle around the top of Dave's head, then resume the same position on the other side. With sleep a non-negotiable, Dave had little option then but to move the cat into a more comfortable zone lower down the mattress.

Dave was delighted with the cat, perhaps because he'd never before had one to call his own. At the same time, he was always aware of the creature's advanced age, that its days were numbered. He'd stare at Gwyn and remind himself - *any day soon he could be gone, and I will miss him*. Then he'd remember the terms on which he had chosen the old cat rather than the ginger kitten and repeat the mantra to himself. *When he goes, I go.*

In an odd sense, then, Gwyn was a kind of clock winding down his own life. Yet, having rediscovered through the cat not a zest for life, but at least a contentment, Dave wondered if he would go through with his plan when the end inevitably came. As time passed, it became an abstract speculation rather than a pressing question - and pass it did. Weeks became months and even years: one, two, then three. Finally, well into the fourth year, Gwyn became ill. He became unwilling to walk or jump, to perform his usual visitations round the neighbouring flats, and even lost interest in food, unheard of for the normally gluttonous cat.

Dave delayed it a while, but at last took him to the vet when the cat's condition became undeniable. Kate was no longer working there, but a new girl showed him through to the consulting room. Dave took Gwyn out and placed him on the table. As the vet, a young Scottish woman, inspected the cat, Dave was afraid to look at her face for he knew what was coming. At last she looked up at him with a sad expression.

'It's his kidneys.'

Dave closed his eyes. It was as he'd feared.

'That's terminal, isn't it?'

'We could try him on medication but that's only delaying it. If we'd caught it earlier, maybe - but he's pretty far gone.'

'So that's it then.'

'I'm sorry. There's nothing we can do.'

Dave looked down, stroking the cat, aware of its bones beneath the soft fur.

'I'll just take him home for one more night, then bring him

back tomorrow. Is that OK?'

'Of course. I'm sorry we can't do anything for him.'

Dave drove home with Gwyn and sat with him through the night, talking to him, trying not to upset the cat by becoming too emotional. That could wait until after tomorrow. Dave tried to stay calm, gently stroking his fur, thanking him for having been part of his life. He offered Gwyn a saucer of milk. The cat attempted a couple of tired laps, as if to please him, then gave up and lay quietly on the bed.

The next morning, Dave took the cat back to the vet. He put his hand behind Gwyn's head and held his little paw as the vet injected him. Soon, very soon, the cat's eyes closed for the last time.

Dave left as quickly as possible, wanting to get away, but realising there was nowhere he could really go that was any better. *So this is how life ends*, he thought. *Not with any fanfare, but in a quiet street on a mundane Tuesday afternoon.*

In his flat later that night, Dave poured himself a large Scotch and looked at the photo of Gwyn he'd just put on the wall.

'Do you know what day it is?' he said. 'March 27. The fourth anniversary of taking you home.'

He smiled sadly.

'You know what that means? I've cracked the four year mark. Took me a lifetime but I finally did it. Thanks to you.'

A tear rolled down his cheek.

'Not only that,' said Dave. 'You kept me alive.'

His old mantra came back to him. *When he goes, I go.* What of the dark promise he'd made to himself four years ago? Perhaps he should honour that now. Then again, such a choice was final and life still had its small pleasures. Maybe he should have taken the ginger kitten after all. It was too late now.

A thought occurred to him. *Either way, what does it matter?*

I'm old... and I don't care. Today, next week, next year, five years... it's only a matter of time. And so what? What does it really matter?

There was an odd sense of liberation in the idea. He'd always taken life so seriously - and for what? *Why does a cat live or die? Why does anyone? Why do we strive so hard when we don't even understand why we're here?*

'I don't know,' he said aloud. 'But I'm not afraid anymore.'

He looked once more at the photo of Gwyn, finished his drink, then went to bed.

Hookup Hell

I

Robert Cornbuckle slumped on the bed, clutching his phone. For the umpteenth time that day, he checked his Tinder profile. 'Still no luck,' he exclaimed in tones of devastated disappointment. With a cry of spiritual dismay, he stood up and went to his laptop. He photo-shopped a hot guy's face onto his profile pic, then cast his line into the Tinder wilderness once more. Within minutes, a beautiful young woman named Imogen reached out to him. To his extravagant joy, they arranged a hookup in minutes, as she lived not far away.

The only concern, as he hurried to the rendezvous, was the fear she might be repulsed when she saw his real face. But in their brief phone messaging, he'd clearly specified he was after personality, not looks, and asked if she was OK with that? To his immense relief, she'd said 'yeah whatever LOL.' Still, a nagging voice in his head wondered what would happen when she saw how ugly he really was.

He stopped and texted that he was running late, then popped into a clothing store and bought a black woollen ski mask which covered his entire face except for his mouth and eyes. That should do the job, he thought. Then, stuffing the mask into his pocket, he walked towards the cafe for his date with destiny.

He made a low key entrance, then went into the cafe's bathroom and slipped on the ski mask. In the mirror he saw his own head covered in a black woollen sock, with just little holes for his eyes and his mouth. It felt quite snug. Satisfied, he walked back out to the cafe's front room and saw a girl working on a laptop. At least, he *thought* it was a girl, due to her body shape, but he wasn't entirely sure because she was wearing a black woollen ski mask on her head.

'This is a bit of a *faux pas*,' he said as he sat down. 'You're Imogen, I presume.'

'Megan,' she replied. 'I'm waiting for my date.'

'Oh,' said Rob, jumping up from the chair. 'I do apologise.'

He made a rapid exit, then walked through to the courtyard out the back - and there she was, sitting at a table under a tree, staring at her phone. The girl was even hotter than the profile pic he'd seen on Tinder - a stunning beauty with straw-blonde long hair. He adjusted the ski mask and approached the table.

'Imogen?' he said, a friendly smile lighting up his unseen features beneath the ski mask.

She looked up from her phone.

'Yes?' she said coldly.

'It's me, Rob.'

'Oh,' she said. She glanced back at her phone, which he now saw was displaying his Tinder pic with the hot guy's face photo-shopped onto his body.

'May I join you?' said Rob, sitting down at the table.

'What's with the... ?'

'Sorry I'm late.'

'The mask?'

'The what?'

'On your head.'

He put his hands to his face, as if in surprise.

'Wow, I've really done it this time. Sometimes I'm so engrossed in analysing the stock market I get dressed automatically without realising what clothes I've put on.'

'Are you going to take it off then?'

'Oh, it's there now - may as well leave it.'

'You look like you've just held up a liquor store.'

Rob laughed, slapping his thigh.

'Held up a liquor store! That's what I want - a girl with a sense of humour. Look, I'll come clean. I'm just finishing my experiments into invisibility.'

This drew a blank look.

'The Invisible Man,' said Rob. 'You know? The movie where the scientist turns himself invisible and binds up his body like an Egyptian mummy so people can see him. You haven't seen the invisible man? Not many people have!'

He slapped his thigh again, then realised he was trying too hard. Better cool it.

'Are you filming? Is this some kind of reality TV show?' said Imogen.

'No, just plain old reality,' Rob replied.

'I'm not sitting here with you wearing that.'

'If it makes you feel better,' said Rob, 'why not leave your phone in your eye line so you can see my Tinder pic. Then you can imagine my face while we're talking.'

Imogen looked at the photo again, then at the ski mask.

'I should probably get going,' she said.

'Imogen, wait,' said Rob. 'I haven't been completely honest with you.'

'Oh yeah?' Imogen said, with a wary look.

'I'm not wearing this mask by accident. You know how I said I wanted personality, not looks?'

'Uh huh,' she replied, glancing round to check her getaway route.

'Then here's the truth. I've learned the hard way how shallow a lot of girls can be. After my last heartbreak, I swore that if I was ever going to find 'the one' she'd have to love me for my personality, not just because I'm a hot guy with a lot of money.'

'Is that right?' said Imogen, relaxing a little.

'Let me give you an example. I've got two cars in the garage.

If I take the Jag to a first date, it attracts the wrong kind of girl. So I always drive my beat-up fifteen-year-old Ford Laser. If the girl still wants to date me, it shows she's not after my money.'

'I'm not into mind games.'

'It's not a game, just a filter to get rid of the phonies. And that's why I'm wearing the mask. What's the point of a relationship based purely on physical attraction? Yeah, it might last a few months, but what about in twenty years when I'm not a male model anymore?'

Imogen's eyes flicked back to the picture on her phone.

'Uh, OK. It sort of makes sense.'

'One thing for sure, I'm not going to find 'the one' with my face. It'll attract hundreds of the *wrong* ones.'

'But I'm not like that. You don't have to wear a face mask for me.'

'Imogen, if you're staring at my face, you won't be listening to my words. I want you to fall in love with my mind.'

'But Rob, what if we want to kiss?'

'We can kiss. Can you not see my lips through the mouth hole in my mask?'

Rob reached out and took Imogen's hand. She stared intently through the eyeholes in his mask, then down at the phone picture again. She shut her eyes and imagined his face.

'As long as you take it off on our second date,' she said, opening her eyes again.

'Too soon. Far too soon.'

'Then how long?'

'I'm very serious about this, Imogen.' He took both her hands this time. 'I'm very serious about you. In fact, I might leave the mask on right up until our wedding night.'

She laughed, but he could feel her pulse speed up a notch.

'You're something else, Rob. I came here for a hookup and you're talking marriage!'

'Do you mind?'

She glanced at the photo again, then back at him.

'You *are* pretty hot and you're not like other guys. I can sense that. But you're not serious about leaving the mask on until we - I mean until you - get married. Are you?'

'Maybe. Maybe not. I'll have to play it by ear.'

'But won't it be a bit weird if we... you know... if we *do* hookup in the meantime?'

'I don't see why.'

She gave a coy little laugh and looked away.

'It sort of turns me on, in a way. The thought of you naked and wearing the mask. You're a real man of mystery.'

'To be honest,' said Rob, 'I don't even want to do the whole sex before marriage thing. Not with you, Immy. I'm an old fashioned guy at heart. When it comes to our wedding night, let's try to retain an air of innocence like there was before this awful hookup culture ruined everything.'

'Oh Rob. You really aren't like other guys.'

He pulled out his phone to check the time.

'And now my love, I must fly. Business calls.'

'When can I see you again?'

'Let us meet in our dreams tonight. Before you go to sleep, say my name three times and blow a kiss heavenwards.'

II

For the next few days, Imogen pursued him online. Robert Cornbuckle deflected her hints and entreaties, which made her pursue him all the more. Rob was oscillating between triumph and turmoil. He'd spent the first night on a heavenly high, certain he was in love. The next day, he realised he'd gotten himself into a bit of a jam over the whole mask business. How long could he keep it on before Imogen saw his real face?

At last in despair, he contacted a dear old friend from schooldays. Emily Turntable was a pal who'd had his back ever since he was bullied in high school. The other kids laughed at them because of their unusual last names. 'Ooh look,' they'd say. 'There goes Cornbuckle and Turntable,' as if the mere possession of a silly three-syllable name was enough to earn their derision. Still, after Emily had dished out a couple of violent reprisals to the ringleaders, the would-be bullies had backed off. Now, at his time of crisis, Rob turned once more to his faithful old pal.

'I've really done it this time, Em,' he confessed. 'I've fallen deeply in love with a beautiful young lady. And I think she loves me too.'

'Really?' said Emily Turntable, failing to keep the surprise out of her voice. 'So what's the problem?'

Rob explained what he'd done, upon which Emily burst out laughing.

'Good one, genius!' she said. 'So what's your next move?'

'I've no idea. That's why I'm calling you.'

'Well, what did you *think* would happen?'

'In hindsight, I didn't really think it through. I was acting on impulse and just thought I'd wing it and hope for the best.'

'You do realise you'll have to wear that mask for the rest of your life?'

'Could I? I did say I'd wear it up until the wedding night.'

'No, dummy, of course not. Look, Rob, were you just after a fling? Did you think she'd take you home and let you do it with the mask on?'

'No, I'm not like that. I was serious about Imogen from the moment I saw her on Tinder.'

'Tinder's not the place to look for your soul-mate. It's just a hookup site, really.'

'Too late. I've found her. I think we're in love.'

There was a silence, then Emily replied.

'Let's be real here, Rob. You're not in love and neither is she.'

'How would you know? You weren't there. The electricity between us was magical.'

'Really? What do you even know about this girl, except that she likes picking up hot guys on Tinder?'

'I haven't known Imogen long, but I'll tell you what I *do* know. She has a lively intellect and an independent spirit. She's as comfortable in jeans as she is in an evening gown. She wants a man who's in touch with his feminine side but can be macho when he needs to be.'

'Did you infer all this from your brief meeting, using your Sherlock Holmesian powers of deduction? Or is that just the crap she wrote on her Tinder profile?'

'One meeting was enough, Em. It was love at first sight.'

'At first sight? She hasn't even seen you! You had a stocking on your head. Let me tell you, Rob, I can predict what will happen when she finds out. She'll act shocked, then disappointed, then she'll get self-righteous and say *it's not your hideously ugly face I mind, it's the lying*. Which itself will be a lie, but never mind.'

'Stop it!' screamed Rob, suddenly furious. 'Stop slandering my girl! We're practically engaged.'

'Fine. Next time you see her, take off your ski mask and get back to me then, you poor, deluded fool.'

With a howl of spiritual anguish, Rob threw away the phone. Emily Turntable was right and he knew it.

'Oh Imogen,' he cried in constipated consternation. 'What will become of our tender love?'

He bent down and picked up the phone from the floor.

'Emily, are you still there?'

'Are you OK, Rob?'

'What should I do, Em? Give me a serious answer please.'

There was a brief silence.

'OK. Here are the likely options in this absurd rom-com scenario you've created for yourself. First, you could keep the mask on as long as possible as a stalling tactic. In the meantime, get a top class plastic surgeon to gradually alter your face so it resembles the guy you photo-shopped onto your profile pic.'

'Oh my god. That's it. You're a genius, Em.' He paused. 'Would it be expensive?'

'What do you think?'

There was another howl of anguish from Rob. His meagre wage as an office clerk would never cover the bills of a top class plastic surgeon whose normal clients were probably all film stars.

'Your second option is to keep the mask on as long as possible and make her fall in love with your mind and personality.'

'Gosh, that's worth a try. Do you think it would work?'

'It's about as likely as the mainstream media reporting the news in a fair and balanced way, but at least it's cheaper than surgery. You know, maybe there's a quicker way. Just show her your real face. You're not that ugly, you know.'

'Oh but I am, Em. I'm hideous.'

'What rubbish. If you weren't so mentally disturbed, I'd make a play for you myself.'

'Emily Turntable, you're too kind trying to bolster the ailing hopes of a lovelorn fool. Counsel me, old friend. How can I win the heart of the fair Imogen?'

'Why not make a fake profile on Tinder using your real face in the picture? Then send her a message and see what she says? Maybe she'll find you attractive.'

'My real face? It's a wild and desperate gambit.'

'At least you'll know where you stand, Rob. If she accepts you, problem solved. If she rejects you, you'll know to keep your face covered for the rest of your relationship.'

III

Eventually, Rob could stall Imogen no more. He bit the bullet and asked her back to the cafe for a second date. He had his ski mask professionally laundered and wore his best pants and jacket, with a red carnation in the breast pocket. He walked into the cafe courtyard, and there she was at their usual table under the tree, staring at her phone. His heart soared like an eagle majestically careering over mountaintops.

'Ah, the girl with the flaxen hair,' he proclaimed with a confidence that eluded him.

'The man in the iron mask,' she parried.

'Debussy,' he said.

'What?'

'*The Girl With the Flaxen Hair*. It's a piano piece by Debussy. I've been listening to it all week, my love. Ever since I met... you.'

'Oh Robert,' she cooed with benign elucidation. 'I know it's Debussy. It's one of my favourite works by the old French master. Topped only by *La Mer* and of course *Prélude à l'après-midi d'un faune*.'

'Imogen, you become more perfect by the moment. To think that you too are a lover of fine music. Who else do you enjoy?'

'Bartok's *Concerto for Orchestra*, of course, along with Stravinsky's *Rite of Spring*. It brings out the pagan whore in me.'

Robert's eyes showed shock through the eye holes in his mask. Then he turned it into a rambunctious laugh.

'You're a wondrous woman of many parts, Immy. Affecting a ribald streak to gently tease me from my lofty aesthetic perch!'

'I do enjoy toying with you, my stallion,' said Imogen 'and taunting you to untapped heights of punishing poetic passion. Yet, if I may allude to another, more recent musical work, you also put me in mind of *Phantom of the Opera*. Tell me, my love, are you hideously deformed beneath your mask?'

'Never!' said Robert with an emphatic snort of derision. 'Take a look at my Tinder profile pic if you don't believe me.'

Imogen stared at her phone, then turned back and took Rob's hand.

'This is yet more playful teasing, my warrior,' she breathed. 'Truth be told, I care not if you have a donkey's behind for a face. Ours is a meeting of the mind and spirit, not the coarse, ephemeral flesh, fickle in its impermanence as it mocks us onward to the grave.'

'Oh my maiden,' cried Robert. 'I see our love has elevated your discourse far beyond the vulgar commonplaces of our first encounter last week.'

'What has come over us, Rob? Could it be we inhabit an altered state of consciousness bestowed upon us by the God of Love?'

'I believe so, Immy. Furthermore, your words embolden me to heights of decisive action of which I barely dared dream, yet prepared for just in case.'

Robert Cornbuckle stood up, took something from his jacket pocket, then got down on one knee.

'Imogen, would you do me the honour of becoming my lawful wedded wife?'

'Oh Rob, so soon. You overwhelm me with your passion, yet confounded by your ardour, I cannot resist.'

'So you consent?'

'If I say yes, will you one day remove your mask?'

'To become your husband, my love, I would remove my own head and lay it at your feet.'

'Then yes, Robert. You will be my husband. A thousand times yes!'

'And now my love, I must fly. My work is done.'

'When can I see you again?'

'Let us once again meet in our dreams tonight. Before you go to sleep, say my name three times and blow a kiss heavenwards.'

IV

Now he was engaged, Robert Cornbuckle, was more unhinged than ever. All his dreams were on the verge of coming true. He'd promised to remove his mask, but that was in the heat of his marriage proposal. No, it must stay on. Yet could he really keep the mask on indefinitely? It was alright in winter, as it was now, but what about when the summer months came around? Besides, could he really trust his future wife? They might be lying in bed together on their honeymoon and curiosity could get the better of her. He'd be lying there asleep in the middle of the night and she'd be tempted to peel back his mask millimetre by millimetre, just for the sake of a quick peek at the man she'd married. Then what? It would certainly make for an awkward conversation at the breakfast table.

He'd better run the fake profile idea, just to see what happened. He logged onto Tinder, made the profile, then reached out to Imogen with a message. 'Hey, I love your pic with the Greek statue behind you. Are you interested in classics?' He pressed send, then flung himself onto the bed in an agony of speculation. Would Imogen accept the approach from his real self? He told himself it didn't matter. If she rejected the fake profile with his real face, he could still court her with his real profile and the hot guy's face photo-shopped onto his body, meanwhile wearing the mask for the rest of his life.

He lay on the bed, fidgeting away. When he could stand it no more, he stood up and went to run a few laps of the oval at a nearby park. When he returned, he saw Imogen had replied to his message from the fake profile with his real face! He texted his friend Emily Turntable. She called back immediately.

'What's up, Romeo?'

'I did what you said, Em. I made the fake profile using my real pic. Now Imogen wants to meet me.'

'Oh my god, that's great! When?'

'Now. She seemed really keen.'

'Then why are you talking to me! Soon as you get home, though, I want a blow by blow account.'

Rob hung up, dressed nicely, then arrived for the tryst at a different cafe to the one where he'd first met Imogen. Soon after he arrived, she turned up wearing the same outfit she'd worn to their first meeting. Robert stood up awkwardly, feeling horribly naked without a full woollen ski mask covering his head.

'Hello. Imogen, is it? Nice to meet you.'

'You too, Pete,' she replied, using the name he'd adopted on his fake profile.

'Do you live around here?' he asked.

'A couple of blocks away,' she said.

'That's handy,' he observed.

'And my flatmate's away for a couple of days,' Imogen said. 'That's even more handy.'

There was, perhaps, an insinuation in the remark. Imogen seemed a bit wound up. Rob found it strangely discomforting.

'I don't care much for this awful music they're inflicting on us here,' he said. 'I'd prefer something a little more refined. Some Brahms, or perhaps... Debussy.'

'Yeah,' she agreed. 'It's hard to talk, isn't it. Maybe we should get out of here and go somewhere quieter.'

'Perhaps the art gallery,' said Rob. 'The Impressionists exhibition is still on. I checked before I came out.'

Imogen shrugged.

'Look, Pete, I don't want to be rude, but can we cut the small talk?'

'I hardly think discussing Impressionist art is small talk. Big talk, more like.'

'Big, small, whatever. I'm not really here to talk, know what I mean?'

'Then why *are* you here?'

'What do *you* think? I haven't had much physical exercise for a while. I need a workout buddy, if you know what I'm saying. The type you can do in the privacy of your own home.'

'But Imogen, I want to get to know your mind. I think we might have a real rapport.'

She looked away for a few seconds, then back at him.

'You know what, Pete? I already have a few people in my life for intellectual conversation. That niche has been filled. If you really want to know what's on my mind, come home with me and I'll show you.'

'Oh,' said Rob. 'I see.'

Imogen raised her eyebrows.

'What's up? You look a bit weird.'

'I am a little... surprised. I didn't expect this to move so fast.'

'What are you doing on Tinder then? Are you coming or not?'

She stood up, took his hand, and led him out of the pub. Rob tagged along, not sure how to process the chain of events. They walked a couple of blocks, then Imogen turned and began kissing him on the lips. He was slow to respond, then began to reciprocate. Imogen's hands found the small of his back, then began to travel south. At that point, Rob pulled away.

'Imogen, what are you doing?'

'What do you think I'm doing?'

'We've only just met?'

'And?'

'I can't, Imogen. Not like this. It's all happening too fast.'

'What your problem?'

'I don't want to do it on the first date.'

'It's not a date, it's a hookup.'

'Not for me.'

'Then why are you wasting my time?'

Rob backed away.

'I'm sorry, Imogen. I'll message you later.'

'Don't bother!'

Robert Cornbuckle turned and ran off in a state of exasperated perplexity.

'Loser!' she called out after him.

VI

'Emily,' he said on the phone, after relating what had happened. 'What am I going to do now?'

'Open the champagne, by the sound of it,' Emily replied. 'She saw your real face and still wanted you. Perfect outcome.'

'But Immy's engaged. To me.'

'Well yes, she's engaged to someone with a ski mask on his head. Now she wants to have sex with him too. Happy days.'

'I'm so confused, Em. What do I do?'

'One thing's for sure. Now you've carried on like a complete klutz, you'll have to keep that mask on for the rest of your life so she doesn't find out it was you. Oh the irony!'

'Oh no. Just when I thought we'd made a breakthrough. So I really have to wear it permanently now?'

'No, you fool. There's only one thing you can do now - fess up. You'll have to come clean about who you really are. With some luck, you'll both have a good laugh about it before the weeding. Ah, I mean the wedding.'

'Gosh, my love life really is the stuff of a Hollywood rom-com, isn't it?'

'More like a French farce. Anyway, you'd better see it through - and as soon as possible.'

'Tomorrow night, then. My whole future depends on it.'

'Good luck - you maniac.'

VII

The next night, wearing the mask once again, he met Imogen at their favourite cafe for dinner. She looked radiant in a black dress, a jewelled pendant hanging from her lovely neck. He drew in a sharp breath of bewitchment when he saw her, and reached down to kiss her gloved hand through the mouth-hole in his face mask.

They chatted their way through the entrée, speaking of matters both thoughtful and socially conscious, as befitting a betrothed couple. In their loving chat, they touched upon Elizabethan poetry, Keynesian economic theory, and the textural homogeneity of Polynesian sculpture. Reassured by their easy chat, Robert took Imogen's hand.

'I do enjoy intercourse with your mind, my love,' he said.

'Do you now?' said Imogen, with a flirtatious laugh. 'As long as that's not the only part of me you enjoy it with.'

She put her hand to her mouth in a coy little gesture, then speared an oyster from her plate, tilted her head up and to the side, and placed the oyster onto her tongue in a wanton manner, glancing sideways to view his reaction through the eyeholes of his mask.

'Imogen, please. This is a public venue. Let's try to keep our discourse appropriate.'

'Oh loosen up, darling,' she replied. 'You really are awfully stiff at times. Oh dear, did I just say that?'

Again came the coy hand to mouth gesture.

'Imogen!'

'Why, Robert, I do believe you're blushing beneath that mask.'

'How much wine have you drunk?'

'Not enough, and neither have you. Let's order another bottle. Waiter!'

'Steady on, Immy.'

'Look, Rob. I know our marriage is a wonderful meeting of minds, but one can't be cerebral all the time. A girl has needs, you know. Frankly I'd like to take you home and rip that mask off along with the rest of your clothes.'

'Have you been listening to Stravinsky?'

'Or leave it on. I don't care. Just take me home.'

'What about our vow of chastity before marriage? What about our meeting of minds?'

'Oh bugger that.'

Robert adopted a sober expression, unseen beneath his face mask.

'I've a confession to make, Immy.'

'Oh really? A good one, I hope. Have you been naughty, Robbie? Do tell Immy.'

'It's serious, I'm afraid.'

'Let's have it then. As the actress said to the bishop.'

'I've been having serious doubts about our marriage.'

'What? I thought you said you were madly in love with me.'

'I was. I am. Desperately in love.'

Robert bowed his masked head and put it in both hands. At

the moment of crisis, his true nature came out, and he uttered a fulsome sigh of baffled bewilderment.

'Goddammit. Never in all my born days have I known a more confounding woman than you, my dearest. One moment I'm high as Mount Everest, the next as despondent as a forest dwelling rodent with no tail.'

'What on Earth are you talking about, Robert? It's not like you to be so melodramatic.'

Rob was about to let out a howl of bewildered bamboozlement, but checked himself so it came out as a small squeak of minor dismay.

'Oh good lord,' he said. 'I love you more than life itself. But damn it, Immy, I've reason to believe you've been cheating on me.'

'Cheating on you, Rob. That's absurd. Cheating on you? With whom?'

Robert Cornbuckle sat up straight in his chair, placed a hand upon his mask.

'With whom? By Cupid's tiny penis, I'll tell you with whom. With me, you lying strumpet!'

And with one firm hand, he tore the ski mask from his head, and flung it aside where it landed in someone's asparagus soup. He stared his fiancée directly in the eyes.

Again, Imogen put a hand to her face. This time the gesture was not coy, but defensively confused.

'You,' she said. 'You?'

'Oh Imogen, how could you?'

'How could I what?'

'I thought our love was pure and would last forever. But as soon as my back was turned, you whored yourself out to the first pretty boy you met on Tinder.'

'Well, Robert. You made me wait so long to consummate our love. A girl can't wait forever.'

'This is our third date. We only met two weeks ago.'

'We may be engaged, Robert, but it's your own fault. I told you I'm not into mind games, but here you are with a mask on your face courting me to the point of marriage, and also cheating on yourself with me using your real face. What are you, some kind of weirdo?'

'I thought I was too ugly for you, Immy. That's why I wore the mask.'

'You're not ugly, you imbecile. We could have had it all if you hadn't cheated on me.'

'*You* were the one who cheated. Don't try to put the blame on me, faithless wench.'

Imogen took the ring from her finger and slid it roughly across the table towards him.

'What are you doing?' gasped Robert. 'Our first fight and you want to throw our marriage in the trash. So I *am* too ugly for you, after all.'

'Oh, Robert. It's not your face that bothers me. It's the lying. Go and find some other girl on Tinder.'

And with that, she stood up and stormed off with nary a backwards glance. Robert threw back his head and howled at his abject folly, and the love that had flared up so briefly like a struck match on a windy night. He ran out of the cafe, on the way throwing his entire wallet at the cafe proprietor to cover the bill (it later counted out to $765 dollars), and ran until he could run no more. Then his phone rang.

'Well?' said Emily Turntable.

'It's over,' Rob said forlornly. 'Imogen's broken our engagement.'

'Oh no. Do you want to talk about it?'

'No, Emily Turntable. We will never speak of this. Not until the scars have healed.'

'Sometime next week, then. That's about how long your last

heartbreak took to mend.'

'What are you talking about?' said Rob.

'Olivia, wasn't it? Sometime last month. You got engaged to her too, remember?'

'Good lord, you're right. I'd forgotten all about her. My word, Emily, I should take up cards. Lucky at cards, unlucky in love. That's how it goes, isn't it?'

'So they say. In the meantime, why don't you come round for a beer and we'll listen to some music?'

'As long as it's not Debussy.'

There was a brief pause before Emily replied.

'Debussy's not the only composer, you know. He may have written *La Mer*, but he's not the only fish in it.'

'In what?'

'The sea, Rob. The sea.'

And with a sigh of penitent relief, Robert Cornbuckle hung up. His old pal was right. She was a dem fine woman, Emily Turntable. Perhaps one day... I mean, who knows? Could it be the answer had been right under his nose the whole time? Was it conceivable that one day his old school chum might be Emily Cornbuckle-Turntable? I mean, she did have a scintillating intellect, a wry yet compassionate nature, and enormous breasts. He raised a quizzical eyebrow at his own folly, then chuckled in whimsical abnegation.

'Too soon, Cornbuckle. Too soon. Don't you ever learn?'

And with a frenzied and rueful laugh, he put his hands in his pockets and continued on his way.

Badminton Boy

I

Badminton Boy woke up grumpy. As he got dressed for work, he frowned at the day ahead. An ocean of evil to be fought, and he had to waste time on yet another meeting with his superhero colleagues. He should be out there catching crims, not having these dumb meetings where they sat around arguing half the time.

He walked into the kitchen, where his girlfriend, Wendy, was making coffee. 'Morning Stuart.'

Badminton Boy winced. 'Please, Wendy, I'm on duty. Am I not wearing my uniform?'

'Sorry, Badminton Boy, you weren't wearing the mask.'

'By the hammer of Thor, Wendy, must I wear my mask at breakfast?'

Badminton Boy was a bit touchy about his superhero uniform. Although it was pretty smart, he felt it lacked a certain something. White shorts and shoes, light-blue sports shirt and socks. Without the mask, he could have been any neatly-dressed guy going to the gym. So, on uniform related matters, he tended to overreact.

'Toast?' said Wendy.

'Thanks.'

'Coming up.'

Wendy spun a piece of toast Frisbee-like across the room. Badminton Boy, by now seated at the table, stuck out his racquet and caught the toast on it without his eyes leaving the book he was reading.

'Big day today?' Wendy asked.

'Just another LORH meeting. That should be enough to waste the whole morning.'

'Do you have to go?'

'Yeah, I got that breach notice for not showing up last time. Remember?'

'Oh, bugger.'

'Mark my words, Wendy, I'll not stand for this much longer. It's only a matter of time before I go LWV.'

'What's that?'

'Lone Wolf Vigilante. Take a look at this.'

He held up his book so Wendy could see the cover.

'*Heroes Who Run Like a Wolf,*' she read out loud. '*How To Quit Being a Team Player and Embrace Your Inner LWV.*'

She smiled a quizzical smile.

'Intriguing - and can the girlfriend still hang out with the wolf?'

'Yeah, of course. It's nothing to do with your private life. It just means I get to dump the three losers I work with.'

They exchanged a super kiss, then both went off to work - she to the law firm where she was a senior partner, and he to LORH HQ.

II

Badminton Boy set off walking down the street, racquet in hand and a quiver full of shuttles at his back. He'd left the Minton-mobile in the garage today, as walking kept him fit and he liked seeing the crims fall back in fear when they saw him coming. His beat was the mean streets of the Bronx, one of the toughest parts of New York, but with that badminton racquet in hand he was invincible.

He was a formidable sight in his white shorts and shoes, light-blue socks and polo shirt, and black eye-mask. Yet he was no physical colossus. His build was trim rather than imposing, and he was only five foot nine. As a blond Caucasian, he was a minority at the badminton club he patronised, most of whose members were Korean, Chinese, or Malaysian. Yet all the members lined up to play with him, hoping some of his skills and wisdom would rub off on them. Like the gentleman he was, he rarely abused his superpowers on court, often in fact playing left handed to even up the contest.

It didn't take long before he saw some crims - two gang members trying to shake down a high school kid for cash. Badminton Boy whipped out a couple of shuttles from his quiver - a regular and a pepper spray - and smashed them towards the thugs. The regular shuttle knocked the cigarette out of one gangster's mouth, and the pepper shuttle clocked the other guy in the face. Whipping round in surprise, the two Bronx thugs took in the fearsome sight of Badminton Boy reloading. Instantly, they cried out in terror and ran off like dogs! With a wink at the bullied kid, Badminton Boy walked on. To celebrate a job well done, he stopped at a café for a cappuccino and read some more from his book, *Heroes Who Run Like a Wolf*.

Chapter Three - There's No I in Team, Cos I'm Out of Here Losers

If you're anything like me, you always knew you were better than the rest, and you're fed up being held back by the goons you work with. But how do you break it to the team that you're going solo? Given your greater emotional sensitivity, it'll be hard on you to have to dump the sorry asses of the colleagues who've latched onto you. So how do you let them down gently without breaking their hearts and having to deal with their bullshit tears and recriminations?

Sometimes, passive aggression is the kindest solution. Be like Ghandi, famous leader of India. Instead of going to war with his British imperial masters, he sat down in the road like a jerk until he irritated them enough that they granted Indian independence. Take a lead from Ghandi and try to be more irritating at work, so they'll want you out of there. This will free you to go LWV.

Yet sometimes this process can take weeks or months, particularly if your workplace has strict wrongful dismissal laws. If you don't have patience for the long game, a policy of being more directly obstructive may be useful.

Yes, of course you could just quit, but that makes you look like the bad guy and may jeopardize any payout which could help launch you into an LWV lifestyle.

III

About an hour later, Badminton Boy stopped reading and walked the remaining short distance to the League of Racqueted Heroes HQ. Or the LORH for short. The H was silent which allowed the team to say 'We Are The LOR' in loud, obnoxious voices.

The other three members - Tennis Tyke, Squash Sonuvabitch and Ping Pong Pow - were already waiting. Badminton Boy was about to apologise for being late but when he saw Tennis Tyke frowning at his watch, he turned it into a boast.

'Pardon me, boys. Had to foil a couple of robberies while you were checking your emails. Now I'm here, we can get started on the real work.'

Tennis Tyke, a tall, tanned American, tightened the grip on his tennis racquet, and the ball he'd been bouncing began bouncing a bit higher.

'Some of us were here at 8am working while you were poncing around in your little white shorts out there.'

Tennis Tyke also wore shorts but they were a masculine black, and quite long. He paired these with a yellow shirt and a rather unnecessary Roger Federer style yellow headband

'Cool it, guys,' said Squash Sonuvabitch. 'Let's not start fighting among ourselves when there's so much crime on the streets. We're a team, right? Let's act like one.'

Squash Sonuvabitch was a nuggetty Korean, equal parts diplomat and street fighter. His real name was Jun-seo, but he'd grown up as 'James' at his American school. Jun-seo's immigrant parents ran a 7-Eleven in the heart of the Bronx, and he'd lost count of the number of times crims had come into the store to rob them. Since the age of five, the plucky kid was often behind the counter helping out, and he'd lived in fear for years until the fateful occasion of his twelfth birthday.

Jun-seo had received an expensive new squash racquet - a gift his hardworking parents had scrimped and saved to afford. He'd taken the racquet proudly to school that day, then put it behind the counter at 4pm when he began his eight hour shift in the shop.

Barely ten minutes had elapsed when a thug came in with a knife, demanding cash. At first, the young Jun-seo shivered in fear and moved to hand over the money. Then something changed. The new squash racquet 'spoke' to him and made him clinically insane. He picked up the mystical squash racquet and beat the crap out of the thug, who dropped his knife and ran off.

Ever since that day, Jun-seo had beaten up countless thugs who tried to flout the majesty of the law. Yet to his credit, he always tried to reason with them first. He was a peacemaker at heart. Unfortunately he was also possessed of a hair trigger temper and if the peacemaking didn't work, plan B was a little conversation between racquet and crim. For now, though, he was in peacemaking mode.

'Come on, guys,' he said. 'Let's kick off the meeting with the ceremonial salute.'

Badminton Boy and Tennis Tyke stopped scowling at each other, and the four superheroes stood up and took positions north, south, east, and west. Four racquets were raised aloft from four right arms. A tennis racquet, a squash racquet, a badminton racquet… and a tiny ping pong paddle. Badminton Boy and Tennis Tyke smirked at each other, their rivalry forgotten as they united in a bullying alliance against the most feeble member of the team. Luckily, as Ping Pong Pow was only four foot high, he didn't see them smirking. If he had, there would have been fisticuffs as he was a tough, wiry Irishman who was always ready to pick a fight with anyone taller than him - which was almost everyone.

'We… are… the… LORH!' proclaimed the four voices in boastful unison. A few high fives went down to round off the self congratulatory vibe of team spirit, which on a good day could last as long as five minutes. But today wasn't going to be a good day. Tennis Tyke cleared his throat.

'Gentlemen,' he said in an officious voice. 'I've prepared a PowerPoint presentation with the agenda for today's meeting so I move we proceed without further delay.'

'Who put him in charge?' Badminton Boy asked the room at large.

Tennis Tyke ignored him.

'As I said, some of us were in here at 8am working while

others were out there allegedly foiling robberies. Someone's got to show some leadership round here. Now I'm going to get on with the presentation I've prepared. Hit the lights, Badminton Boy.'

'Don't order me about, you jerk.'

'By the power of the strings just do it!' said Squash Sonuvabitch. 'Must we have this constant bickering?'

'Hey, watch your language,' protested Ping Pong Pow.

Squash Sonuvabitch swore under his breath. This was an ongoing issue. The quartet had until recently been a trio calling themselves the Lords of the Strings instead of the League of Racqueted Heroes, but when Ping Pong Pow won his legal appeal to be allowed to join the group, they'd been forced to change the name. Squash, tennis, and badminton racquets all have strings, while a table tennis paddle does not. So any mention of strings touched on their tiny colleague's frail sensitivities.

The three of them thought it was bloody stupid. A table tennis bat is technically not even a racquet, so they had no idea how the decision had been made to allow him in just because his game was a bit like theirs. But for some reason, the Executive Council of Superheroes ruled against them and let their vertically challenged friend into the group.

Tennis Tyke had been particularly opposed to it because their new member wanted an alliterative super name based on 'table tennis' rather than ping pong. Tennis Tyke said no way and insisted on a P name not a T name - which led to the faintly ridiculous moniker, Ping Pong Pow. The original three looked down on him as a noob and an imposter. Behind his back they made fun of his tiny paddle, which they considered a laughable superhero weapon. Sensing their condescension, Ping Pong Pow had the habit of constantly challenging one or more of them to duels of honour.

'I do apologise,' said Squash Sonuvabitch. 'I won't mention strings again, as I don't want to cause tension by reminding you that your superhero weapon has no strings and is only six inches long.'

'That's another offensive string-themed word right there,' said the prickly Irishman. '*Tension*. You can't help lording your damned strings over me. How about we settle this Dublin-style, squash boy?'

For a moment, Squash Sonuvabitch felt the red mist arising. Then he controlled himself.

'How about we just start the meeting? Get the lights Badminton Boy.'

'*Jawohl herr commandant!*' said Badminton Boy. 'What's next on the agenda - invading Poland?'

'Look, if you don't turn off the lights within five seconds I'll apply to have you issued another breach notice.'

Badminton Boy, remembering his wolf book's advice, got up all passive-aggressive and walked towards the light switch in exaggerated slow motion. When he finally reached it, he turned towards his crime-fighting colleagues with a mischievous glance.

'Hey fellas, an impression. Guess who I am? No wait, I'll tell you. This is Tennis Tyke's girlfriend turning on a light switch.'

Badminton Boy bent slightly at the knees and just as he pressed the light switch, emitted a guttural grunt at colossal volume, like a female tennis star serving at Wimbledon. Tennis Tyke stood up and raised his racquet.

'Want to take this outside, Shuttle boy? Let's sort this out once and for all. Oh that's right - your tiny shuttlecock might blow away in the wind.'

'Hey, it's not my fault your girlfriend can't do the simplest things - like serving a little ball over a net - without grunting like a brontosaurus on heat. I'd sure hate to live with her and hear her going to the toilet or something.'

Tennis Tyke smashed a tennis ball at 150km per hour in the direction of Badminton Boy, where it missed him by a few inches and rebounded way over to the other side of the room.

'Fault,' commented Badminton Boy. 'Why don't you try a second serve and slow it down to half speed like you do on court, pussy?'

Tennis Tyke threw up another ball and smashed it at 160km per hour this time. Badminton Boy swatted it away just in front of his face. Tennis Tyke ran across the room and the two superheroes faced each other, racquets in hand, like old style swordsmen ready to duel to the death. Squash Sonuvabitch had seen enough.

'Fellas, will ya grow up already? Here we are in the Bronx and we're meant to be fighting crime - but we're fighting each other over who has to turn off a light switch. Now listen up - we're going to start the meeting and, so help me God, the next guy who's out of order will have me to answer to. You two clowns shake hands.'

Badminton Boy and Tennis Tyke laid down their super weapons and sulkily shook hands.

'Finally!' said Squash Sonuvabitch. 'Right, Tennis Tyke, before I give my presentation, would you like to add any business to today's agenda?'

'Sure. We need to discuss your name.'

'Sorry, what?'

'Your name, Squash Sonuvabitch. The Executive Council of Superheroes has had a few complaints. Parents think it sets a bad example for kids. You can't have a superhero name with swearwords in it.'

'Didn't we have this out already? I'm not changing my name again. First I was Super Squash. You said that was stupid, so I changed it to Mr Squash before Ping Pong Pedant over there said only the villains have Mr in their names. Finally I come up with a tough super name and you're still not happy!'

'The name isn't that tough, you know,' said Badminton Boy.

'It is so.'

'Not really - it's dumb. It's like me calling myself Badminton Badass or something stupid like that.'

'Or Tennis Tough Guy.'

'Or Ping Pong Powerhouse.'

'Yeah? Well, guess what guys? I'm not changing my name again. It's Squash Sonuvabitch and you can take it or leave it.'

'In that case, you'll be issued a breach notice and you can take it up with the Executive Council.'

'Then I'm quitting the group.'

Squash Sonuvabitch stood up and violently overturned his desk so a stack of papers went all over the floor. He smashed one of his squash balls at the front window of their HQ so hard the glass shattered into a thousand pieces.

'Wait,' said Ping Pong Pow. 'You can't quit the group or Badminton Boy and Tennis Tyke will kill each other within minutes. We need you to balance them out or nothing will ever get done around here.'

'You should have thought of that before,' said Squash Sonuvabitch. 'Let's see how you idiots get on without me. I've been reading this awesome book about going LWV, and I guess the moment has come.'

'Hey, I've been reading that too,' said Badminton Boy. 'No way you're quitting before me. Alright, you can keep your name, Squash Sonuvabitch, as long as you stick with the team.'

'Well... maybe I'll give you guys one more chance,' his colleague replied. 'Quitting's kind of a big step.'

'You know, guys,' said Tennis Tyke. 'The problem is we lack leadership. We're all on the same rank, so without a hierarchy there's no chain of command and nothing ever gets done. We need a leader. As has been shown by the events of the last few minutes, Badminton Boy and Squash Sonuvabitch lack the maturity to take charge, so I'm going to have to reluctantly take the job for the greater good of us all.'

'Great plan,' said Badminton Boy. 'The only problem is it's about as likely to happen as squash being televised on prime time TV.'

'Much as I resent that remark,' said Squash Sonuvabitch, 'I'll pretend I didn't hear it so I'm not forced to destroy this entire building. I'm going to calmly propose a counter solution. The fact is us three have a love-hate relationship. We fight like brothers and none of us will ever bow down to the others. So I propose Ping Pong Pow for our leader.'

'What!' exclaimed Tennis Tyke. 'But our racquets are nearly two foot long and he's only got a tiny little ping pong paddle. There's no way he can lead us.'

'Would you rather elect me or Badminton Boy?'

'No way.'

'Then why not Ping Pong Pow? He can be a sort of Yoda figure. Tiny and pathetic in stature, but powerful beyond his looks.'

'Watch it, pal!' said Ping Pong Pow. 'That's the second time you've insulted me today.'

'I said you were powerful.'

'And pathetic. I'm no Yoda.'

'Yes you are. You're barely four foot tall.'

'OK, big fella, let's settle this here and now. I challenge you to a duel.'

'I accept. Let us choose our ammunition and settle this like men.'

'Very well then.'

Squash Sonuvabitch selected one of his best black rubber squash balls. Ping Pong Pow in turn selected a white table-tennis ball. As both balls were placed on Tennis Tyke's desk for inspection, it was clear they were almost exactly the same size. One black, one white, both deadly weapons in the hands of their respective masters. It was a daunting sight, at least until a gust of wind from the window blew the white ball off the table and onto the floor.

Now he was again in an official position, Tennis Tyke was in his element.

'Gentlemen, take your weapons and positions.'

Holding their racquets, Squash Sonuvabitch and Ping Pong Pow stood back to back in the centre of the room, took ten paces counted out by Tennis Tyke, then spun around and belted their balls at each other.

It was a meeting of primal forces - black against white, evil against good, thick rubber against thin lightweight celluloid. The two balls collided in mid air and the ping pong ball smashed to smithereens. But as neither racquet-wielder was directly hit, there would have to be a replay.

The second time, Squash Sonuvabitch took his ten paces again, but the cunning Ping Pong Pow took only baby steps this time. On the count of ten, both heroes spun around, but Ping Pong Pow ducked, and firing from close range, was able to hit his target this time. Squash Sonuvabitch's missile, however, went firing wildly over his opponents head... where it rebounded against the back wall and came back to strike the prematurely triumphant Ping Pong Pow.

IV

At that moment, a siren went off in the LORH HQ. A crime alert! Badminton Boy picked up the phone and with a wink at his colleagues, began to speak.

'You've dialled the League of Racqueted Heroes. Please listen to the following prompts, as our menu options have recently changed. If you'd like to report a robbery, please press one. For murder, press two. To dob in a drug dealer, please hit three. For any tips on where I can score some blow, hit four. If you're a badminton groupie, don't hit any numbers, just show up at the door. If you have a complaint, find a therapist in your area and have a good cry. If you want... oh, it's you Police Commissioner. Beg pardon, George. Just trying to do my bit for team morale. By being a complete ass, you say? Well, you're entitled to your opinion, but... Quite frankly, I don't care for your tone. You don't have any authority here, Commissioner. Watch it pal. Anyway, what do you want? A holdup at Crookshanks Restaurant on 47th street? That's robbery then. Why didn't you press one? Look, I'll check our schedule and see if we've got time to save your sorry ass again.'

Badminton Boy put down the phone.

'Right, lads, hold up on 47th. Let's skip the ceremonial salute. Better get straight over.'

The four crime fighters sped over to 47th street. The scene was worse than imagined. The area had been cordoned off and cleared of the public. Gazing up to the window of the third floor restaurant, they could see one of the robbers had taken a hostage and was holding a knife to his throat. A bunch of cops were standing by, staring up at the troubled scene.

'Afternoon Inspector,' said Tennis Tyke. 'Give me a briefing.'

Before the cop could reply, Badminton Boy shouldered his way in front of his rival.

'Afternoon Inspector,' he echoed. 'Give me a briefing.'

As if used to this sort of thing, the officer addressed them both.

'Seems to be a hostage slash burglary situation with terrorist overtones,' he said.

'I see,' said Tennis Tyke. 'An HSBSWTO, eh. Tricky.'

'What do you guys recommend?' the cop said.

Squash Sonuvabitch stepped into the frame.

'If I recall,' he said 'the standard response to an HSBSWTO is a 32B. That means I blast the knife out of his hand with a squash ball, while my colleague Tennis Tyke whacks a couple of tennis balls at the crim's head. Then Badminton Boy will run inside and free the hostages while we take the scum into lawful custody.'

'Sounds watertight,' said the cop. 'And what about... the other member of your team? The little one.'

'Oh - Pee Pee? He can do the paperwork afterwards.'

The three members of the formerly named Lords of the Strings shared a bullying chuckle, at which their height-challenged chum had finally had enough.

'That's it, you guys. You can shove your paperwork. I'm going to take out these bozos on my own.'

And with those angry words, Ping Pong Pow ran recklessly into the building, wielding his paddle like a tiny club of vengeance.

'Oh great,' said Tennis Tyke. 'That could be a spanner in the works of the old 32B. What now?'

'Leave him,' said Badminton Boy, with a sly look. 'It's not so bad if you think about it. Room full of armed crims, hot-headed kamikaze dwarf who wants to prove himself. Whichever way it goes, it's win-win.'

The three superheroes paused for thought, until Tennis Tyke spoke up.

'Bags not doing the paperwork if he goes down.'

'Bags not either,' said Squash Sonuvabitch.

'Hey, not fair,' said Badminton Boy. He thought for a second. 'Right, 32B. Let's go.'

The heroic trio took up their positions. But just as Tennis

Tyke and Squash Sonuvabitch were poised to unleash their deadly balls of doom, there was a commotion at the window and both the criminal and hostage disappeared from sight.

'What the hell?' said Tennis Tyke in annoyance. 'Maybe the little jerk pulled it off. Better get in there boys.'

The three racquet wielding heroes ran into the building, where they were met with a most unexpected sight. The six gang members had been disarmed and were now being restrained by four other individuals, all of whom the team recognised with considerable annoyance.

'The Bat Brigade?' said Squash Sonuvabitch. 'What are you idiots doing here?'

V

A tall, bespectacled chap answered him. His name was Cricket Cad and he was dressed impeccably in cream trousers and shirt, topped by a blue England blazer.

'The Commissioner called us,' he said loftily. 'Said he offered the job to you chaps, but Badminton Boy carried on like a complete ass on the phone. so he told our lot to come and do the job properly.'

The Bat Brigade was a team of rival superheroes. A sort of Charlie's Angels, they consisted of three badass modern female heroes - Lacrosse Lassie, a Native American; Baseball Bitch, a tough Puerto Rican girl; and Hockey Hardass, an Islamic Canadian who wielded a hockey stick from behind a burka. Cricket Cad himself was an arrogant Englishman who deliberately spoke down to the LORH boys whenever their paths crossed. The present situation was a prime opportunity.

'I say, Badders,' he said. 'Be a good chap and fix me a gin and tonic. I do believe our work is done.'

Badminton Boy crossed his arms.

'You bitches have got no business here. This is LORH territory.'

'Fancy that,' his nemesis replied. 'I was having a chat with the Commissioner and it looks like your team's being relocated to a low-crime neighbourhood. Somewhere more suited to your abilities. Meanwhile, the Bat Brigade are taking over the Bronx.'

'You English jerk. They don't even play cricket in America.'

Cricket Cad raised his cricket bat slightly.

'I dare say that when it comes to facing the might of our arsenal, the insular citizens of the Bronx are in for a little cultural exchange. Am I right, sisters?'

The pompous and conceited Bat Brigade laughed loudly and raised their weapons. Lacrosse Lassie held up her racquet, Baseball Bitch wielded her bat, and the fearsome burka-clad Hockey Hardass shook her stick.

'Love your little white shorts, Badminton Boy,' said Baseball Bitch. 'Want to turn round and give us a twirl?'

At this Tennis Tyke stepped in.

'You can't say that, Baseball Bitch. This is a workplace and that's harassment.'

'Shut up, Tennis Tit. You're not giving any orders around here.'

As usual, Squash Sonuvabitch, was obliged to step in as peacemaker.

'Look, guys. There's been a bit of a mix up. It's Badminton Boy's fault for being a jerk on the phone, and I can assure you he'll be getting an official breach notice. But this is our turf and your team will have to go. Now, surrender those crims into our custody so we can take them in.'

'Shan't,' said Cricket Cad. 'Now shove off.'

'I'm going to count to ten,' said Squash Sonuvabitch. 'Then

it's on.'

'Go ahead,' said Lacrosse Lassie. 'I'm going to count to ten in Iroquoian first.'

'Huh?' said Squash Sonuvabitch.

'That's her Native American tongue, you ignoramus,' said Baseball Bitch. 'In a show of solidarity, I will join my crime fighting sister by counting to ten in Spanish. And Hockey Hardass will count to ten in Arabic.'

'Oh yeah? Bring it on bitches.'

He turned to his three LORH colleagues.

'Boys, are we going to let them count to ten before us? Come on, let's show 'em what we can do. Hey, they started without us. That ain't fair! Right, that's it.'

And it was on. The four members of the LORH drew their weapons and began to fight. Tennis Tyke served a ball in the direction of Cricket Cad, who hooked it away with his bat. Squash Sonuvabitch smashed a black ball at Lacrosse Lassie, who caught it in her net.

Meanwhile, Badminton Boy and Baseball Bitch were locked in mortal combat, while Ping Pong Pow went toe to toe with Hockey Hardass. As the carnage went on around them, the hostages cowered under restaurant tables, and the six criminals ran out the back door to freedom, until only the two crime fighting teams remained inside battling fiercely over the right to maintain order in the Bronx going forwards.

For long minutes the battled raged with neither crew able to gain the ascendancy. Then, in a caddish manoeuvre, Cricket Cad snuck up behind Badminton Boy and clocked him with his cricket bat. Badminton Boy dropped his racquet and tottered beside the open window of the third floor restaurant.

'I say, Baseball Bitch,' said Cricket Cad, 'Let's finish this chump off, shall we?'

With a cruel laugh, Baseball Bitch, took a baseball out of her arsenal and made ready to pitch it. She took aim at Badminton Boy's forehead, knowing a direct hit would knock him out of the window and to his doom on the footpath below. Yet no sooner had she thrown the pitch that a tiny enraged dwarf intervened. With a cry of 'nooooo,' Ping Pong Pow threw himself in the path of the ball. In so doing, his tiny frame absorbed its full impact and he fell to the ground, mortally wounded.

With a cry of rage, the three remaining LORH boys saw what happened and rallied. They charged upon the Bat Brigade with such fiendish ferocity that their enemies gave up and beat a retreat out of the building. Badminton Boy, Tennis Tyke, and Squash Sonuvabitch raised their racquets and cheered. Then they turned back to face their fallen brother, Ping Pong Pow, still lying on the floor. Tennis Tyke was first to speak.

'Come on, old sport. On your feet.'

'Yeah, come on,' said Badminton Boy. 'I'm going to buy you a beer. I owe you one, pal.'

But their colleague lay still.

'Sorry, fellas, I'm not going to make it,' he croaked. 'But raise a glass for me tonight.'

'Stop clowning, Pee Pee,' said Squash Sonuvabitch. 'You're MVP today for sure. You've finally proved yourself. Welcome to the team, champ.'

Ping Pong Pow seemed not to have heard him. He was fading fast.

'All I wanted to do was fight crime. Ever since I came up as a kid on the mean streets of Dublin. And gentlemen, you made that dream come true.'

'This is only the start, kid,' said Tennis Tyke gently.

'I tried to join their gang,' Ping Pong Pow continued. 'The Bat Brigade. But they laughed at me. Told me my table tennis bat wasn't a proper bat. Who's laughing now?'

The tiny hero coughed for several seconds. His LORH

brothers began tearing up as they realised he was a goner.

'You saved my life, Pee Pee,' said Badminton Boy. 'You can't leave us now.'

'Yes, my brother,' said Ping Pong Pow. 'I would do it again. For while the Bat Brigade rejected me, you boys accepted me into the team and made a young Dublin kid's dream come true. God bless you all.'

And with that, the tiny crime fighter expired. His three LORH brothers bowed their heads in solemn respect.

'He was the bravest of us all,' said Squash Sonuvabitch.

'He can never be replaced,' said Badminton Boy.

'We will never forget him,' said Tennis Tyke.

The three LORH boys raised their racquets in a final salute.

'We. Are. The. Lor!' they shouted.

'Right,' said Badminton Boy. 'Who's for pizza?'

'Roger that, Bad Boy,' said Tennis Tyke. 'Let's dial in two large Pepperonis with olives and a bottle of Coke.'

'Who put you in charge?' said Squash Sonuvabitch. 'I'll have a seafood and a bottle of Pepsi.'

'Hey guys,' said Badminton Boy. 'Let's get both. We've earned it.'

And on that note, the crime fighting trio shook hands and went on their merry way - the Lords of the Strings once more.

The Tightarse Tuesday Book Club

The Tightarse Tuesday Book Club met on a Wednesday. Their real name was the Stromborne Heights Book Appreciation Society, or SHABS. Once a month they got together over a drink to celebrate their love of literature.

July had been the group's fourth anniversary, yet Lorna Graham was a bit down. What should have been a big do had turned out a fizzer when only six members showed up. Six! At the height of their reign, the club had pulled in twenty members on a good night. Who could forget that time thirty-one people showed up for the reading of John Silvern's *Dog Face*? The next day, a smug Lorna had sent out a notice that numbers would be capped at twenty-five from now on, or else the club would have to find a bigger venue.

Of course, she had no intention of leaving the Smugglers' Arms Hotel. Not only was it a comfortable harbour-side venue only five minutes drive from her home, there was the all night 'happy hour' with ten dollar cocktails and gourmet pizzas every Wednesday. Indeed, Lorna had made it part of the package. For fifty bucks a month, you got two cocktails, all the pizza you could eat, and a brand new copy of the book they were reading next. Not a bad deal. Book club night was almost the highlight of Lorna's month. Good friends, books, a couple of drinks - what more could you want?

So what could explain the decline and fall of the Stromborne Heights Book Appreciation Society? Attendance had been dwindling for some time, but last month was rock bottom. She'd sent out that cute email with pics of balloons and champagne glasses, trumpeting the SHABS 4th BIRTHDAY BASH! What an embarrassment when only that meagre half dozen bothered to show up. She'd had to resort to extra cocktails, then snuck the car down side streets to avoid the cops on the way home.

The next Saturday morning, she popped into The Phantom Pheasant coffee shop. As she waited by the counter, she caught sight of her reflection in the mirror. Roots were showing a bit - time for a trip to the salon. Other than that, she wasn't looking too bad. Not many forty-five year olds would have the confidence to flirt with the young barista, as she'd just done while ordering.

She turned to the back of the cafe and spotted Trev and Tilly at a far table. She was pretty sure it was them. Stocky Trev with his bald head and slim Tilly with her mop of dark brown curls. Tilly's head seemed to bob down rapidly behind the menu for a second. Then it re-appeared as she waved in exaggerated fashion.

'Lorn!' she said, when Lorna had wandered over. 'Come and sit down.'

Lorna took the offered chair, so that Trev was on her left and Tilly on the right. Gee, Trev had put on some weight since the last time she's seen him.

'Guys, where've you been hiding?' said Lorna. 'SHABS has missed you. Especially last week.'

'How was it?'

'Terrific. Really nice. Although, once again, we did miss some of the old crew. Come to think of it, we haven't seen you since March. Where've you been?'

'Oh you know,' said Trev. 'Busy, busy.'

'Always on the go,' said Tilly. 'So much to do, so little time.'

'Anyhoo,' said Lorna. 'I thought to myself, *is it me? Did I do something wrong?* Maybe I've been choosing the wrong books. Is that it?'

Tilly looked at Trev, then back at Lorna.

'Well look, Lorn, if I'm honest, I've got to say SHABS

started to get a bit pricey for us. Ever since you made it fifty dollars for the night.'

'We're mortgage slaves now,' said Trev. 'And we do have our trip to think of.'

'South America,' said Tilly. 'November.'

'Goodness,' said Lorna. 'How exciting. But aren't you worried about all those poor people? It could be dangerous.'

'We're with a tour group,' said Tilly. 'Quality hotels only.'

'And that's not cheap,' said Trev. 'We've got to be a bit sensible now. Can't go throwing money about like we used to. Ah, food!'

A waiter arrived at the table and gave an Eggs Benedict to Tilly and a Big Breakfast to Trev.

'More coffee?' the waiter asked.

'If you insist,' said Trev. 'Large cap with one.'

'As long as you know you're welcome back anytime,' said Lorna. 'We can probably cut costs. Maybe you can just buy the book. No one said the pizza and drinks should be compulsory.'

Tilly's face showed little enthusiasm.

'No offence, Lorn, but it won't be much fun sitting there while the rest of you are quaffing cocktails.'

'And pizza,' said Trev. 'I mean, we've all got to eat - and even mortgage slaves deserve a night out once in a while. Hey, how about this: why not get rid of the book?'

Lorna laughed, and touched Trev's arm.

'That's what I miss about you, you old wag. Always good for a joke.'

'I'm serious,' he continued. 'Just make it a social night. I mean, we all love reading but, you know.'

Lorna stopped laughing.

'Well, gee, Trevor. We are the Stromborne Heights Book Appreciation Society, not the pizza appreciation society.'

Trevor put down his fork and picked up his coffee mug.

'I know, Lorn. We're all book lovers here. Dammit, why does everything cost money? If only we could have all this without paying.'

'Hang on,' said Tilly. 'Any chance the Smugglers' Arms will throw in the pizza for free? Or give us a cocktail on the house?'

'Come on, Tilly,' said Lorna. 'It's already happy hour. They've got to make *some* money.'

'Oh bugger them,' said Trev, shoving a sausage in his mouth. 'They buy those liquor bottles by the crate. A little squirt in the glass and they're hitting us for a tenner. Outrageous. The customer gets shafted every time.'

'And those pizzas,' said Tilly. 'Probably cost them two dollars each to make. Gourmet pizzas, indeed!'

'As I said, Tilly, the food and drinks are entirely optional. Just come for the book.'

Tilly speared a portion of smoked salmon and egg with her fork, and brought it to her mouth.

'Sorry, Lorn, but I don't see why we have to miss out just because we're mortgage slaves. If you think Trev and I are going to sit around and watch everyone stuffing their faces with delicious pizzas and cocktails, well, that's not much fun for us, is it?'

Lorna raised her eyebrows.

'Maybe you should ask the Smuggler's if they'll lay on a spread for free. You never know, they might go for it.'

Tilly stopped eating and thought deeply for a moment.

'Look, how about this?' she said. 'Of course we want to keep the book - we're all book lovers here - but why do we have to buy it? I've heard of plenty of other book clubs that don't.'

Lorna looked doubtful.

'It's true not all clubs buy the book. I just thought that we are SHABS, you know, the Stromborne Heights Book Appreciation Society, and we're all book lovers here.'

Trev and Tilly nodded, then intoned together.

'We're all book lovers here.'

'So I just thought,' Lorna continued, 'it doesn't hurt to give something back to the author who created the book in the first place. Give them their fifty cents a book, or whatever the royalty is.'

'Fifty cents?' said Trev. 'That's pathetic!'

'It's quite funny,' said Tilly. 'So if twenty of us go to book club, that author would make ten dollars out of the night. That's enough to buy one of those gourmet pizzas!'

'Oh, it might be more than fifty cents,' said Lorna. 'Maybe it's two dollars. Anyhow, it's not much. At least we're giving something back to the author.'

Trev put down his fork and wiped his mouth.

'Look Lorn, we've all got problems. I am not here to subsidise authors. I know we're all book lovers here, but if authors are silly enough to enter a low paying profession like writing, that's their look out. I've got my mortgage to pay.'

'Gee, Trev, maybe some of those authors have a mortgage too.'

'Oh really?' said Trevor, with a smirk. 'Most of them are probably living in mansions like JK bloody Rowling!'

Lorna raised an eyebrow. 'I hardly think using the world's richest author to represent the rest of them is very fair.'

'I hope Trev doesn't mind me saying this,' said Tilly, 'but we spoke to a financial consultant a while ago. Guy named Richie. Bloody genius, wasn't he, Trev? Apparently he used to go round businesses and get rid of excess staff who were costing too much. Not just tin pot businesses either. Banks, corporations, you name it. Apparently he shut down an entire department at Sydney University. Not enough students enrolled, so he closed them down.'

'I see,' said Lorna.

'Anyhow, he doesn't do that sort of work anymore. Doesn't have to, if you know what I mean. But we met him on a cruise and he did us a favour. We had a little chat about how to save money. Didn't even charge us, did he, Trev? Thing is, he made us think about our spending, then he showed us how much we were wasting on stuff we didn't need to buy.'

'That's right,' said Trev. 'I mean, we're all music lovers here, but I used to almost be an addict when you think about it. I had a $1200 a year habit - that's how much I was spending on music. Richie showed me how to cut ninety percent of that. You know what I spend now? $120 a year on a streaming service and I get all the music I want. I can still be a music lover, but it only costs me ten bucks a month!'

'Ten bucks?' said Tilly. 'That's how much it costs for one of those cut price cocktails at the Smuggler's Arms.'

'Outrageous, isn't it!' said Trev. 'They buy those liquor bottles by the crate. Geez, the customer gets shafted every time.'

'Goodness,' said Lorna mildly. 'Sounds like musicians aren't getting much back if you're only paying ten dollars a month for all that music. And the streaming company will be taking a fair chunk of that.'

'Those musos get their cut, Lorn,' said Trev. 'Besides, we've all got problems. We're all music lovers here, but if those guys are silly enough to go into a poorly paid profession like music, that's their look out.'

'Sounds like Richie would endorse that philosophy,' said Lorna. 'But what if all the musicians go broke? Maybe we won't get any new music.'

'Doesn't matter,' said Trev. 'There's already so much music, we don't need any more. And here's the brilliant observation Richie made. He said those creative types have a compulsion to create and a need for recognition, so they'll keep doing it anyway even if they don't get paid. All the better for us, eh?'

'Anyway,' said Tilly, 'getting back to book club, we don't mind coming back as long as you cut costs. I know we're all book lovers, but there's no need to waste money when we don't have to.'

'What do you suggest?' asked Lorna. 'Borrow from the library?'

'Perhaps,' said Tilly, not looking keen. 'That's one idea.'

Trev leaned over, uncomfortably close to Lorna. She could feel his breath in her ear.

'I hope Tilly doesn't mind me saying this, but she's a bit of a germaphobe.'

Tilly winced.

'Well, *anyone* could have handled those books. Probably reading them on the loo, for all we know. Disgusting!'

'I never thought of that,' said Lorna with a shudder. 'I suppose you won't want us to buy a couple of copies of the book and take our turns passing them on?'

'That's not quite so bad,' Tilly replied. 'At least I'll know what sort of people have been handling it.' She frowned. 'As long as I can have the first turn.'

'I know,' said Lorna. 'Ebooks! They're much cheaper. That should get the budget down.'

Trevor sighed.

'If you don't mind, I spend quite enough time looking into a screen all day at work. I'm not going to come home and do it some more. I prefer a hard copy, thank you very much.'

'Oh for God's sake,' Lorna said. 'Do you have any suggestions?'

'I've got one,' said Tilly, raising her hand. 'Giveaways. It won't cost us a cent.'

'What do you mean?'

'There's all these competitions, Lorn. You've got no idea. Until Richie told us to cut our entertainment spending, I never knew. Once I looked into it, you wouldn't believe all these book giveaways there are.'

Tilly uttered a nasty laugh.

'All these struggling authors are so desperate for publicity, they have to literally give their books away for the sake of a free online review. But if they think I'm going to be a soft touch, they'll find out different. Only last month I won a free book in a giveaway. Did I care for the book? Sorry, try harder, and stop wasting my precious time. After two chapters, I tossed it in the trash. I gave him a review alright - one star out of five!'

Trevor smirked.

'She can be a bitch sometimes, but you've gotta love her.'

He leaned over and planted a wet kiss on his wife's cheek. Meanwhile, the waiter came over with the bill. Trevor glanced at it and raised both eyebrows.

'Geez, that's what breakfast costs these days, is it? The customer gets shafted every time. Anyhow, these book giveaways sound like a good idea.'

He laughed.

'Supply and demand working in our favour for once. So many books, so few readers. No wonder authors have to kiss our arses these days.'

'I thought you said they were all living in mansions like JK Rowling,' said Lorna.

'Eh? Well, not straight away. They've got to pay their dues first. No such thing as a free lunch, right?'

'And certainly no free pizza and cocktails at the Smuggler's Arms,' said Lorna.

'Then stop making us pay for the book,' said Tilly. 'If you do that, even the mortgage slaves will be able to show up.'

'So you guys will come back to SHABS?'

'Sure,' Tilly replied. 'We're all book lovers here. Just show us a little compassion. It's not much to ask.'

A light bulb went off in Lorna's head.

'Hey, how about this? Let's say we schedule books three months ahead. Then I'll buy one copy for every ten readers and we take turns. Give everyone one week to read it, then pass it on. That way it will only cost everyone about two dollars each.'

'Two dollars! Why should we... oh, OK, I suppose it's not much. After all, it's nice to give a little something back to the authors. I do like to support authors.'

'Throw them a few crumbs!' said Trev.

'It's only right,' said Lorna. I mean, at two dollars a book, that's really only twenty-four dollars a year, isn't it? So you guys will come back to SHABS? I've missed you!'

'OK, Lorn,' said Trev magnanimously. 'Long as we don't have to pay for the month we're in South America. I don't see why we should pay an extra two bucks if we won't be at the meeting.'

'And by the way,' said Tilly, 'Trev and I are married so we sort of only count as one person, right?'

'Oh,' said Lorna. 'You want to pay only $24 a year between you? That's going to make it more expensive for the other members.'

Trev put a noble hand on his wife's shoulder.

'Never mind. We'll pay separately. We do love to support the arts.'

'We're all book lovers here,' Trev, Tilly, and Lorna all intoned together.

Lorna stood up.

'I'm delighted to hear it. I look forward to seeing you guys back at SHABS next month.'

So there it was. From a chance encounter in the Phantom Pheasant cafe, The Stromborne Heights Book Appreciation Society was reborn as the Tightarse Tuesday Book Club. By the time the fifth anniversary came around, membership was booming again. Everyone came to the party at the Smuggler's Arms and stuffed themselves with pizza and cocktails - and not one person complained about the two dollar fee for buying the book. Mighty big of them. After all, we're all book lovers here!

Toileport

Oh, what a perfect morning. The sun shone down on the city of Sydney, blessing all who dared chase their dreams. Here is the story of one of them: a man with values who would not be swayed from his vision.

His name was Stephen E. Carone. With a spring in his step, he surged through the doorway of the Felicity Fry Literary Agency. He was pleased to see that Felicity was alone at her desk. She was a scholarly looking woman in her forties, kindly, but with a hard business head - which is why she spent most of her time on her successful clients. She was even now reading through a press schedule for a visiting writer from overseas. Therefore, the unexpected visit of a minor local author was not a thrill but a distraction. To this, that author was oblivious. Taking the chair opposite, and skipping the formalities, Stephen beamed and handed her the manuscript.

'I know I'm not supposed to bind them ahead of editing, but I just like the way it looks and feels in my hand.'

She looked at him warily. Or was it wearily? It was both. As she took in the gangly, yet dapper, fellow in front of her, she wondered what was in store for her this time.

'Hello, Stephen. So this is the new book you mentioned last week. It's a surprise, I must say. Why didn't you tell me before?'

'For that very reason. It's a surprise - to me as well as to you. But who am I to argue with inspiration when it strikes? I wrote the whole thing in three weeks.'

'I see. But I'm still trying to place your last book. Nothing has been finalised there. You know that.'

'Sure, but rather than sit around waiting, isn't it better I get ahead of schedule and come up with something new?'

Apart from a small pursing of the lips, Felicity kept her face expressionless. It was always one extreme or another with these author types. Either they had writer's block and couldn't come up with anything or they gave her multiple projects at once, like a litter of puppies. Then she was expected to find homes for them all.

'What is it this time, Stephen, fiction or non-fiction?'

'Fiction,' he beamed. 'Fiction based on fact.'

'It would really be a lot easier to place your work if you could stick to one genre. Find some sort of niche for yourself.'

'You said that last time - but why should I limit myself to one little niche?'

'Publishers don't want someone who jumps from topic to topic. They can't market it. And bookshops don't know where to place your books either, they can't find the right niche in their shelves.'

'Oh very good, Felicity, you've just literalized a metaphor.'

'And you've verbed an adjective. But really, Stephen, you mustn't forget the readers. One doesn't like to confuse them. I mean, what if Agatha Christie, along with her two hundred crime novels, had turned out a science fiction book?'

'Well done, Agatha, if you ask me.'

'And you, Stephen, you're supposed to be a science writer like Richard Dawkins. Richard's very successful in that genre - but what if he decided to branch out into teen romance? Would that work?'

'Excuse me, Felicity, but maybe we authors don't have to be one dimensional beings. What happened to the good old days of the polymath, the person who's accomplished over a variety of fields? Polymaths were very highly thought of in the nineteenth century. Everything's about specialization now, isn't it? More's the pity.'

Felicity mused briefly. The polymath. It was probably a bit retro. Then again, retro was very now. Perhaps Stephen could be branded as a polymath, and they could aim for the polymath niche in the market. It would be a lot of work though and mightn't pay off.

'This isn't the nineteenth century, Stephen, it's the twenty-first. I told you last time - if you want to make a career, get with the times. For your own good, I'm going to be brutally honest. The literary world isn't an intellectual playground, it's a marketplace. Stephen E. Carone isn't an author, he's a brand. If we want that brand to be viable, we need a target demographic so we can begin niche marketing in a fiscally responsible manner going forward. For a start, make a decision - are you a fiction or a non-fiction writer? Then, it's best if you can choose one specific genre and concentrate on that.'

'Why can't I do both fiction and non-fiction?'

'I told you. It's confusing for publishers, booksellers, and the public alike. We need something more focused. Frankly, I hope you stick with non-fiction. It's much easier to sell.'

'How are you going with *Zero Minus One*? That's non-fiction.'

'Your book on the origin of the universe? To be honest, I'm having trouble selling it. You know, I'm not sure people want to read that super sciency stuff anymore. It was big in the nineties. Stephen Hawking and all that, but Hawking had the right image. Unless we can put you in a wheelchair and give you some kind of terminal illness, disability, or similar branding gimmick, you won't make a dent in the public consciousness.'

'Oh come on, Felicity, my book's much better than Hawking's. He makes a joke in the first paragraph on page one, but the rest is pretty much unreadable. I don't think even one percent of the punters got past the first chapter.'

'That's all the more reason they won't be buying *Zero Minus One*. No publisher wants to touch pop science at the moment.'

'Well, that's lovely, isn't it. How many years did I spend

writing that book? Now I have to wait for Hawking's curse to wear off.'

'Anyway, Stephen, while you're here, tell me about this new book.'

Carone's scowl lightened.

'Ah, *Zoronta*. It's a futuristic thriller set in the past. It's about a small group of rogue scientists who try to make a physical simulation of the internet. They create a virtual world that interacts with the real world so that in the end no one is sure which is which. They concoct a physical version of Google in order to transport themselves around the virtual / physical world. But then control of the technology falls into the hands of a US political group who use it to try to go back in time and prevent the September 11 terrorist attacks. The scientists realize this will create a historical paradox that could destroy the world, so they also travel back in time to try to stop the rival group.'

Felicity Fry, drummed her fingers quietly on her desk for a while, before eventually speaking.

'Wasn't that time paradox thing already done in *Terminator*?'

'Sure, but it's not like *Terminator* invented that sort of plot. The old time travel paradox has been around since science fiction was invented.'

His agent looked unconvinced.

'Apart from that, I'm not sure we should touch September 11 just yet. It may be a bit too sensitive.'

'It's been over fifteen years.'

'Finally, this thing about the characters Googling themselves around the virtual world. It sounds a bit like a teleport, wouldn't you say? And you know what I told you last time about teleports, don't you?'

'It's not a teleport. It's a virtual Google.'

'A Googleport?'

'If you like.'

'I told you, Stephen. You're a good writer, but I don't understand this bizarre preoccupation with the concept of teleportation as a means of transport. Every year you come into my office with some variation of the idea. I mean, why? What is so great about teleportation? What's wrong with a car, a plane, or a train for heaven's sake?'

'That's exactly it. On the train, you're crowded together with strangers, you can get mugged, you can miss your stop. With the teleport, I could be beamed straight from your office to my home in an instant.'

A wishful look appeared on Felicity's face.

'Planes are no good either,' Carone continued. 'They're so slow. It takes a day to cross continents and two days to recover. With a teleport, I could be overseas as quick as snapping my fingers.'

'But there *are* no teleports, Stephen. It's nothing to do with reality, it's a complete fantasy.'

'The absence of teleports from our world is all the more reason I should write about them and raise public consciousness. You said you wanted me to specialize, to fill a niche. Why don't I specialize as an author of fictional and non-fictional works on the theme of teleportation?'

'Because no one cares. People only care about real things, day to day things that matter. The price of petrol, for instance.'

'The price of petrol will plummet as soon as the teleport is invented.'

'For God's sake, Stephen, you're not breaking any new ground here. Teleportation has already been done. *Star Trek*. *Doctor Who*. Harry bloody Potter! Just leave it. Think about something else to write about.'

'But I've already written *Zoronta*. Won't you at least read it?'

Felicity shrugged.

'Leave it here and I'll have a look - but I really think it's time you moved on to some other subject matter. Try to think of it as teleporting away to a new topic area, if that makes it easier for you. Look, I was thinking about it last week, and I might have an idea for you to consider. But only if you take that sulky look off your face.'

'I don't want to.'

'If you refuse to listen, I'm afraid I can't help you.'

'What, then?'

'Are you ready to be open minded?'

'Try me.'

'Now, before I say it, let me warn you it's a bit of a change of direction. Perhaps a little more lowbrow than your usual stuff - but at least there might be an audience for it.'

'Oh God. What is it then?'

'Toilets.'

'What?'

'Why don't you write about toilets, poo, and so on? There have been a number of hits in this area. In the Australian market, at least.'

'I find that hard to believe.'

'What about the movie, *Kenny*, for example? The one about the portaloo guy. A massive hit, internationally as well. You could write a book like that. Then there's Andy Griffiths, the children's author who writes those books about bums and bum related topics. A literary icon for Australian children. Why don't you write something like that, but suited for the adult market?'

'I've just written a book about the origin of the universe.'

'As I told you, Stephen, people don't have time for that highfaluting intellectual stuff anymore. They don't have the concentration. Let's be frank - no publisher wants to touch your science book. But in the wake of *Kenny* and Andy Griffiths, they *will* touch poo.'

'What about my Google teleport?'

'Look, you need to move on from that teleportation crap. The origin of the universe is out. Teleportation is out. Poo is in. I've found a niche for you, now it's up to you to fill it. What do you say?'

'Gee, Felicity, I don't know. I've put all this time into *Zero Minus One* and *Zoronta*, and now you want me to write about toilets.'

'I'll admit it's a change of direction. But you know, I've been in this game a long time and I've got a funny feeling you could pull it off. I've a nose for this sort of thing.'

'So this is what my PhD in physics has come to.'

'Why don't you get an academic job?'

'I want to be a writer.'

'Then all I am saying is give toilets a chance. If you have a hit, maybe you can go back to your more intellectual work. In the meantime, unless you come up with a better idea, I'm not sure we should work together anymore.'

'Like that is it? Alright - I'll see what I can do.'

Toileport

By Stephen E. Carone

Chapter 1

Lucas paused at the end of the castle corridor. There was no one about. No knights, no servants, and definitely no royalty. Most of them were preparing for the imminent attack of St Ninian's men. Furtively, Lucas entered the castle's primitive latrine area where his Toileport was hidden. If only he could get back to his own time before they were overrun by armed marauders. Surely his present fear and desperation might even work to his advantage. Yet as he sat down with a fervent will, the opposite seemed to have happened. His bowels seemed to have constricted rather than loosened, and try as he might, he just couldn't crap himself to safety.

Oh why had his bowels deserted him in his hour of peril? His arse had always been so reliable in saving itself, yet this unprecedented crisis of constipation had left him in the lurch.

Lucas's ears strained desperately to hear what he thought might be St Ninian's men scaling the castle walls. It was probably only his imagination, yet prompted by the sense of danger, his life flashed vividly before him. The days as a child prodigy, the triumphant final school exams at eleven and the scholarship to Cambridge at twelve. Then, a few years later, his doctoral thesis on quantum physics and time travel. The initial skepticism of his professors giving way to grudging acceptance and admiration. Then, the low point of his life when he'd been asked to address a conference of scientists, only to find his water bottle spiked with drugs by a jealous rival, and his subsequent mortifying meltdown at the event. He'd been humiliated and made into a laughing stock.

That had led to an obsessive need to regain credibility, which led to eighteen hour work days until finally the ass-tonishing breakthrough.

Lucas remembered it like yesterday. He'd fallen asleep in the bathroom of his lab after another long and fruitless day. He'd been in a state of fevered dismay at the lack of progress trying to solve the question of the wave-particle nature of photons, and even resorted to a couple of shots of rum to drown his sorrows. Drunk and exhausted, he'd gone to use the toilet before going home, but had passed out on the bathroom floor. Well, that was all in a day's work, but when Lucas awoke, he found that he'd somehow travelled back in time a week.

It was only with the aid of his prodigious intellect that Lucas was able, through a gradual process of controlled experiments, to piece together the truth. The astonishing discovery was that Lucas was able to crap himself back and forwards in time. Through a bizarre conjunction of alcohol, poo, and a quantum randomizing machine, Lucas was able to transport himself into the future or past, and around the globe. Somehow, Lucas's bowel movements had become affected by his experiments. Random permutations in the quantum flux, aided by some shitty ripples along Heisenberg's uncertainty principle had given his excrement the ability to propel his body and mind through time. All he had to do was have a nip of alcohol, go to the toilet, activate his quantum device - which he dubbed a Toileport (© Stephen E. Carone) - and excrete, and he would find himself materializing at random points in the space-time continuum.

It was all terribly novel, of course. Indeed it was an extraordinary scientific breakthrough, yet in light of Lucas's previous experience, he wasn't sure he could make it public. Lucas's magnificent ability to poo himself through the space-time vortex might win him the Nobel prize, but there was the distinct chance it could make him a laughing stock once again.

It was the mother of all quandaries. He agonised for several days and nights. Then finally Lucas decided he needed to retain his ability to time travel, but in a less embarrassing way. He resolved to travel back in time to that momentous night, by now about six weeks ago, in which he'd first drunkenly crapped himself into the past. He would then, from a sober vantage point, observe and analyse exactly what had happened that night, and try to replicate the results in a more fragrant and less toilet-esque manner.

It had seemed a simple and logical plan as Lucas fired up the Toileport. Yet intellectual genius is often accompanied by ineptitude on more mundane matters, and Lucas, before embarking, had that day made the rash decision to lunch at a new Indonesian restaurant with a penchant for chilli-themed dishes. By the time he launched the Toileport, there was the distinct capacity for misadventure. Not to put too fine a point on it, at takeoff, the Toileport exploded into action, overshot the mark, and careered wildly off course. It re-materialized in Renaissance Italy, and from there, it had been a wild carousal ride through history.

Since that first misstep, Lucas had made several narrow escapes. Most recently, he'd Toileported himself to the American civil war, witnessed the building of Stonehenge, and escaped imprisonment at the hands of the evil Aztec Queen Papantzin the Third.

Now, Lucas faced perhaps his greatest peril yet. For the umpteenth time, he wished he'd been more of a polymath in his studies, focusing on history and the humanities rather than just physics and esoteric maths. That way, he might have known more about the conventions of castle attacks in medieval times. It was now nearly dusk. Did the attacks generally occur at night under cover of darkness (in which case he was likely to be slain before his constipation eased)? Or did the marauding forces generally wait until dawn and the hours of daylight, (in which case, he still had a few hours to somehow coax a lifesaving excretion from his inner being)?

All he could do was hope for the latter. Yet he still desperately needed to trigger a bodily evacuation in order to activate the Toileport. A thought occurred to his prodigious intellect. He would have to revert to induced diarrhoea. There was no 20th century chemist product to aid his struggles, so he'd have to improvise. He would have to go to the castle kitchens and hope against hope he could find some item of food which had gone off, which would in turn send him off so that he could escape these hideous Dark Ages and get back to his own time once more. Give or take a hundred years, anyhow.

He found his way to the kitchens and searched with some desperation for food scraps, until finally he found a pile of rotten vegetables in a corner. A rat scuttling away from the pile helped to turn his stomach. *Desperate measures*, he told himself, and stuffed a handful of the vegetable matter into his mouth while trying hard to ignore his natural aversion. He took a big gulp of medieval wine to kill the taste.

It didn't take long before Lucas felt something coming free, yet at that very moment there was a ruckus from higher up in the castle. The first of St Ninian's men had just managed to scale the walls and battle was joined. It might only be minutes before they were here, swords in hand to slay all the inhabitants.

Lucas rushed to the Toileport and sat down. An armed knight charged into the room and raised his sword to slay him with a single blow, and the mortal terror of that moment did the job. With a great rush, the Toileport exploded to life and sent him careering through the space-time continuum once more. Oh, where would this journey end? Only time would tell.

Stephen E. Carone lay back, satisfied, reading over the chapter he'd already sent to Felicity. She'd probably have read it by now - and speak of the devil, there was his phone going off. The name Felicity Fry came up on the screen. In eager excitement, he pressed the green button.

'Hello,' he said.

'Stephen? We need to talk.'

Dr Why and the Attack of the Social Justice Warriors

Introduction

This story is a satire of the TV program, *Dr Who*. To those who don't watch the show, it may not make much sense. To briefly explain: the main character is a time travelling alien called the Doktor. He also regenerates his body every few years, which means a new actor can come in and play the role. At the time of writing the character has, for the first time, changed into a woman. This has caused some controversy.

For this story, I've used the device of including all the character's selves and calling them by the last names of the actors who played them. So, in order: Hartnell, Troughton, Pertwee, Baker T, Davison, Baker C, McCoy, McGann, Eccleston, Tennant, Smith, and Capaldi.

In writing this story, I am obviously not referring to the actual actors, but a fan's perception of the characters they played in the show (although at times that blurs into a perception of the actor too). In any case, whatever I say has nothing to do with the actors in themselves, the use of their name simply designates the version of the Doktor they played onscreen. I have avoided giving any controversial lines to these characters. There is a little banter and parody, but that's all. The more 'controversial' views in the story are spoken by the character named Dr Why, who is clearly someone else, with no direct association with the program.

A few points. First: my story is not very flattering in its view of the Capaldi version of the character. Well, apologies to Capaldi, but I disliked the direction the program took while he was there. This is the fault of the BBC writers and producers more than Capaldi, although as he went along with it he is also partly responsible.

Second: I have no rights to *Dr Who*, so have used no trademarked names. However, under the category of satire and 'Fair Use' I am using this short story to comment on the recent trend in which science fiction films and TV shows are used as a vehicle for 'progressive politics.' This applies not just to *Dr Who* but to other films, TV shows, and superheroes.

There are a number of reasons why this is a bad idea. I won't go into them here, but will simply note that I used to really like *Dr Who* but now actually dislike it.

Third: As a long time fan of *Dr Who*, I am entitled to my views on the program. If *Dr Who* is serious about ethical and intellectual values, it should permit criticism. If, however, it frowns upon criticism and tries to suppress it, it will reveal itself to be exactly the sort of authoritarian regime which the fictional Doktor so often fought against.

Fourth: In the main dialogue, I am obviously discussing much wider issues than just the TV show *Dr Who*, which is merely a symptom of those issues.

Dr Why and the Attack of the Social Justice Warriors

I

Somewhere in time and space, a tall, skinny man walked sheepishly into his spaceship. He was followed by a tiny and beautiful girl.

'I'm so sorry, Cora,' he said. 'I didn't mean to land on the wrong planet and lead us into that den of racist armed mercenaries. Thank Heavens you were there to beat them up singlehanded with your martial arts skills while I watched from the sidelines.'

'Never mind, Capaldi,' said Cora. 'You weren't to know it was a trap. But you could have lent a hand when I was up against all those racists.'

'Oh dear, I thought it might seem condescending to join in. It might have implied you weren't able to beat up all those men on your own. Well, I'll make it up to you, I swear. I'll make a point of punching out the very next racist I see. In fact, let's go back to England in 1800 right now. The very first misogynist white capitalist we meet is going to feel the wrath of my fisticuffs.'

'Forget it. I'm flying this spaceship from now on. You've messed up once too often. Get me a beer, will you.'

'At once. It's the least I can do,' Capaldi replied, rushing for the fridge. He returned, carrying a brown bottle on a tray. Cora frowned.

'That's not approved brand. It's Bro beer from Texano, that planet run by white slavers. What's it even doing here?'

'Oh gosh. I do apologise. I thought they'd already had the uprising.'

'That's pre-revolution brew, you ignoramous.'

'So sorry. I'll get you something else.'

She raised her hand, as if to slap him. He lowered his head and scuttled back to the fridge, returning this time with a tray holding a bottle of approved beer and some salted peanuts. Yet just as he reached Cora, he tripped, fell, and spilled the tray's contents all over the floor.

'Oh dear, I am sorry,' he stuttered. 'I don't know why I'm so thick all the time. It must be the testosterone particles infecting my brain. What can I do to make it up to you?'

Cora sighed.

'Just clean it up. I'll get my own beer. No wonder you're the last male Doktor.'

II

Back in the distant past, a tall chap with prematurely white hair knocked on the door of the meeting room. The man, whose name was Pertwee, had no idea who'd sent the mysterious summons, but apparently it was urgent. The door was opened by a short man who, by contrast, had jet black hair.

'Oh, it's you,' said Troughton.

'Was it you who put out the distress call?' said Pertwee.

'No, I answered the same message,' Troughton replied. 'If you're here too, that must mean the old docs have been called up for another team effort.'

'Again?' said Pertwee, with a distinct lack of enthusiasm. 'I suppose the other one's here as well.'

'Yes, unfortunately,' said Hartnell, from a comfortable chair at the back of the room. 'We've clearly been brought here for a reason.'

A door opened and a man named Tim Lord walked in. He was from the same race as the Doktors, and had the habit of calling them up to perform vital missions.

'Ah, you've arrived,' he said. 'But where are the rest of you?'

'The rest of us?' said Troughton. 'Surely three are enough to solve any problem.'

'Afraid not,' said Tim. 'We're going to need the whole lot this time. All eleven of you.'

'That's enough for our own football team,' said Pertwee. 'I suppose you want us to use our super powers to win the World Cup for England or something. Is that it?'

'Something much harder. This is probably the worst crisis we've ever faced. That's why we need all of the first eleven Doktors.'

'What about the twelfth?' said Hartnell. 'How come Capaldi gets out of it?'

'Capaldi's part of the problem. He's been kidnapped and brainwashed into working with the enemy. They're controlling his mind.'

Troughton frowned.

'Who are we up against: the Dorleks? The Cyberpeople?'

'Worse. We're under attack from the Social Justice Warriors. One of the deadliest foes known to man - and I use that word advisedly.'

'Can't say I've heard of them,' said Pertwee. 'What's their game?'

'They're a group of secular fanatics out to create a social Utopia by destroying Western civilisation.'

'Why?' said Troughton.

'They're obsessed with the past mistakes of European countries, which they blame on white European men. They're going to fix it and create a world of perfect justice by giving power to everyone else instead.'

Pertwee raised an eyebrow.

'It sounds like an administrative nightmare, to say the least.

Who did you say these people are?'

'The Social Justice Warriors. SJWs for short. Don't underestimate them. They've taken over education, entertainment, and the media to brainwash everyone into pursuing their socially-just dream.'

Hartnell shrugged.

'I don't see why all the fuss. Let their Utopian folly run its course. They'll soon find out it doesn't work, then some other regime will take their place.'

'But they're not just taking over the world. They've taken over all the big science fiction franchises and comic book heroes too - even your own show.'

'In what way?'

'For one thing, all the main characters are turning into women. The brigadeer-general's been replaced by his daughter as head of the military.'

'Justice? Sounds more like nepotism.'

'And the Meister has regenerated into a woman.'

'Oh really?' said Pertwee with a chuckle. 'I'm not sure what he'd think of that.'

'As have you.'

'Oh really!' Pertwee repeated, this time with a frown. 'I'm not sure what *I* think of that.'

'What's the reason?' asked Troughton.

'It's part of their overall plan. The Social Justice Warriors believe power is divided according to basic categories like race, gender, and sexual orientation. They say straight white males have always had all the power while blacks, gays, and women have been marginalised. They're trying to fix this by removing as many white males from positions of power as possible, and replacing them with members of the oppressed classes. That's why you're regenerating into a woman, so your character will no longer be played by one of the oppressor class.'

'I say, that's a bit much,' said Troughton. 'I've staged more revolutions than Trotsky had hot dinners. I've always fought against injustice - and now I'm the villain?'

'Sorry, Doktor, the Social Justice Warriors don't like you anymore. Not unless you stop being a white male. You need to become a woman, black, gay, or something like that.'

At the back of the room, Hartnell stood up and waved his hand dismissively.

'Let them play their silly games. That's the future. I'll cross that bridge when I come to it.'

'I don't think you realise how powerful the SJWs are,' said Tim Lord. 'They've not just taken the future they're trying to rewrite the past as well.'

'Impossible.'

'They're trying to affect the past by sending their influence back through time. Haven't you noticed anything strange lately? Any odd little vibes that seem anomalous to what you're used to? I don't just mean the political stuff, but the entire flavour of new series *Doktor Who* itself.'

'Now you mention it,' said Pertwee, ' there have been a couple of things. The wild mood swings, for example. I mean, one minute I'm going along being totally flippant and jolly, like I don't have a care in the world, and thirty seconds later I'm incredibly earnest, pondering the deep existential tragedies of what it means to be alive. There's no transition, it just happens.'

'Ah yes, Tennant-itus. That's New-Who all over.'

'And why is there sexual tension between my companions?' said Troughton. 'My spaceship used to be a platonic zone, and I was pretty much an asexual being. Now there are strange hints of emotion and sexuality. It's all so unpleasantly adult.'

Tim Lord raised his eyebrows. 'Apparently we *must* have sexuality in everything.'

'As for me,' said Hartnell, 'Why are my adventures becoming

so complicated? They used to be simple enough. Now I can barely follow them myself.'

'You see?' said Tim. 'That's all New-Who. Your program's different in the future, and the effects are coming back through time to you.'

'But why should the future impact the past?' said Pertwee.

Hartnell and Troughton recoiled in horror.

'You used 'impact' as a verb,' said Troughton. 'You could have said 'affect' instead of 'impact.' So it's true! The awfulness of the future really is impacting the past. Oh good heavens, now I've said it! This is appalling.'

'I think you're starting to realise the gravity of the situation,' said Tim. 'And it's even worse than I thought if silly linguistic trends are coming back through time as well. We're going to have to take on the SJWs as a team.'

'Surely the three of us can stop them.'

'Afraid not, old chap, we need the other eight.' He looked at his space watch. 'They should be here any moment. I've got them arriving in chronological order. Baker, T should be here any second.'

There was a knock on the door. In walked a slim, fair-haired young man in cricket clothes.

III

'Davison?' said Tim Lord. 'What happened to Baker, T?'

'How would I know?' said Davison. 'We don't really talk.'

Pertwee and Troughton exchanged a mischievous look.

'While you're here, would you take a look at my pet cat?' said Troughton. 'He's got fur-balls.'

Pertwee sniggered.

'And make us a cup of tea, Farnon. There's a good chap.'

Davison sighed.

'Very funny, gents. Do you have any idea how hard it was going from playing a vet to playing the Doktor? I was pretty tough following you two, let alone Baker, T.'

'What do you mean *let alone Baker, T*?' said Pertwee. 'Are you implying he was better than us?'

Before Davison could answer, there was a knock at the door. Two middle-aged men in colourful suits walked in.

'Well, look who's here,' said Pertwee. 'Baker, C and the real McCoy - the lamo eighties Doktors who got the show cancelled.'

'It's not our fault,' said McCoy. 'You're only as good as your writers and producer. You had a dream team behind you, Pertwee.'

'As I deserved,' said Pertwee haughtily.

'Now we are six,' said Hartnell. 'That's surely enough to defeat the SJWs.'

The door opened and in walked Paul McGann.

'Oh my,' sniggered Baker, C. 'Time to call in the big guns.'

'I was the best Doktor of the nineties!' said McGann angrily.

'You were the *only* Doktor of the nineties,' said McCoy. 'And you made *one* episode.'

'It was a *movie*, not an episode'.

'Goodness,' said Pertwee facetiously. 'I can't wait for the Paul McGann boxed set to come out on DVD.'

Troughton snickered behind his hand.

'It'll probably be director's cut with an extra two minutes of footage. *That'll* be worth a bonus disc.'

'Shut up, you guys,' said McGann. 'It's not my fault they never went on with the show in the nineties. You don't tease John Hurt for just playing the Doktor in one story. Why pick on me?'

'No,' said Pertwee, 'but he played Caligula and the Elephant man. You've got to respect that.'

Next, a tall skinny man in a leather jacket walked in. Christopher Eccleston, the first Doktor of the new 21ˢᵗ century era. He looked pretty pissed off.

'My contract was clear. One series. No comebacks, no specials, no multi-Doktor reunion stories. I saved your arse. Job done. So why am I here?'

Before anyone could answer, two hyperactive young men burst through the door performing a juggling routine.

'Oh look, it's the wack brothers,' said Pertwee. 'Tenant and Smith. They're far too young to play the Doktor.'

'What's wrong with being young?' said Davidson.

'You still here, Farnon? Where's my cup of tea?'

'Righto!' said Hartnell. 'Now there are ten of us. Surely that's enough to defeat the SJWs.'

'Not quite,' said Tim Lord. 'We need the whole team. We need the most powerful Doktor of all. Look, I'll see if I can get through to him.'

He sent out a thought wave and a couple of minutes later, a tall, curly-haired man walked in. He wore a coat and an overlong scarf, and he was playing with a yoyo.

'Baker, T. At last,' said Tim. 'Where were you? Hurry up, we need you to help us defeat the SJWs of the future.'

'I'm sure you chaps can sort it out. Between the lot of you, you should be able to manage.'

'Oh come on Baker, T.'

'Shan't.'

'We need you.'

'I feel like being a twat. I'm going to be difficult for no reason.'

'You owe us one for skipping *The Five Doktors*.'

'If I didn't do it with five, what makes you think I'd join up with this tea party?'

'You're the most powerful of the classic Doktors. We can't win without you.'

Baker, T looked sulky and continued playing with his yoyo.

'Only if you get rid of the other Baker.'

'Baker, C?'

'What on Earth were you thinking hiring another actor with the same name as me, the most famous Doktor? He never stood a chance. And if you think I'm going to answer to Baker T, you're much mistaken. I am Baker. The one. The only.'

Tim Lord turned to Baker, C.

'Terribly sorry, you're fired.'

'Again? Jesus Christ!'

Baker, C ran for the nearest window and threw himself out. The others could hear his death scream fading away as he plummeted to the ground. Tim Lord turned back to the other ten Doktors.

'Right, let's get on, shall we?'

<h1 style="text-align:center">IV</h1>

Back in the future, Capaldi had just finished writing out his punishment lines - 'I apologise for being born and will try to overcome it' - five hundred times in long hand. He was heading back from the SJW supermarket, wheeling a carton of ideologically-sound beer on a trolley, when he heard a noise.

'Psst, Capaldi. Over here.'

Capaldi looked to his left and saw Troughton's head poking out from around a corner. He gasped in shock, then hurried on. With an impatient sigh, Pertwee stepped out from behind the wall, followed by Davison, Tennant, and the rest of the crew.

'What are you chaps doing here?' said Capaldi.

'We're here to stop the SJWs interfering with time,' Davison replied. 'Come with us and we'll fill you in.'

'Oh no, I can't,' said Capaldi. 'I'm already on two strikes with Cora. There'll be a fearful row if I don't get home on time with this beer.'

'Don't be absurd,' said Pertwee. 'You can have a drink after we've stopped the SJWs. Now come with us.'

'I'll just drop this back and see if I can get permission to stay out past curfew.'

Baker stepped forward, grabbed the carton of beer, and threw it over a hedge. There was a sound of breaking glass. Capaldi looked terrified.

'Oh gosh, Baker. You've really landed me in the stew now.'

'Pull yourself together, man,' said Baker. 'Tell us where SJW HQ is.'

Capaldi turned and pointed at the tallest building in the city.

'It's over there. Everyone knows that. You chaps really are the worst. I'm going to have to go back for more beer now, and I'm already late.'

'Come with us, Capaldi,' said Pertwee. 'Help us defeat the SJWs.'

Capaldi went white.

'No fear. I'm not going up against them. The consequences! Oh my, the awful consequences.'

'And what are they?' asked Troughton.

'What?'

'The consequences of defying the SJWs?'

'I don't know, but I sure don't want to find out.'

'Why are you so afraid?' said Pertwee.

'Stop talking to me. You fellows are going to get me in a lot of trouble.'

'So what? Come on, Cap. Let's go.'

'I'm not listening to you people any more. Go away!'

Capaldi stuck a finger in each ear and starting singing 'la la la la la la la,' as loudly as possible. Then with a burst of deranged laughter, he ran off.

'The poor devil's lost it,' said Pertwee. 'Come on. Let's all of us make a plan for how to get into SJW HQ.'

The meeting was a disaster, with ten strong-willed leaders battling to get a word in. The first five Doktors squabbled, Tennant and Smith bounced around like jumping beans, Eccleston stood there with arms crossed looking aloof, while the two Macs sat around like a couple of extras. The arguing was getting worse. At one point Davison had to take Tennant and Smith aside for a 'private chat.'

'I say,' said Davison. 'Could you fellows tone it down a bit? I know you're trying to impress Baker, but he's threatening to quit again.'

'Well, give me a line?' said Smith. 'This is the first time I've opened my mouth in this whole story.'

'What about me?' said Tennant. 'I was the best of the new series Doktors. Everyone knows that.'

'OK, chaps,' said Davison. 'I'll have a word to the others and see what I can do.'

When they returned to the group, Pertwee was holding forth.

'There are just too many of us. There's no way all ten can infiltrate SJW HQ.'

'He's right. Some of us have to go,' said Hartnell.

Troughton drew himself up to his full height of five foot two.

'I vote that anyone whose series was cancelled during their run can shove off.'

All eyes turned on McCoy and McGann.

'You've got a nerve, Troughton,' said McCoy. 'You were on very thin ice during your last year.'

'Until they signed me,' said Pertwee.

'On your way, McCoy,' said Hartnell. 'As for you McGann, you're not even a real Doktor. All you did was make a bad American telemovie! You've got about as much cred as Peter Cushing!'

The two Macs stood up sulkily and walked off. Meanwhile, Baker had pulled Tennant and Smith into a private conference. When it finished, Baker shook hands with them both and they ran off in great excitement, talking extremely fast. Baker returned to the group, dusting off his hands.

'How'd you manage that?' said Pertwee.

Baker looked smug. 'I told them to devise some convoluted method of breaking into SJW HQ. It involves reverse engineering through ten dimensions of time, while using their alien physiognomy in a uniquely gimmicky way of some sort. And while they're distracted by that nonsense, let's just overpower the guards and walk in the back door. We're down to six now. That should allow us to get in without attracting much attention.'

'Make it five,' said Eccleston. 'My contract said one series. See ya.'

'Even better,' said Pertwee. 'And let's not forget someone has to stay behind to make the tea for when we get back. How about it, Farnon? Be a good chap.'

'Fine,' said Davison, 'but stop calling me that. Do I call you Worzel?'

'Splendid,' said Baker. 'So we're back to the original fab four.'

'Make it three,' said Hartnell. 'I can't risk being captured by the SJWs, or I might be roped into Capaldi's regeneration story as a propaganda tool to lecture fans about sexism.'

'Fair enough,' said Baker. 'Looks like it's Troughton, Pertwee, and me then. I'm sure that will be a wonderfully harmonious team with no conflicts whatever.' He opened his eyes wide.

V

The Doktors approached SJW HQ, walked in the back door, overpowered the guards, and reached the command centre with surprisingly little trouble. Indeed the place was deserted, and they were able to walk through unopposed.

'I say,' said Pertwee. 'The SJWs have conveniently displayed their plans in clear written form on that whiteboard up the front of the room. That certainly saves us some trouble!'

'You're right,' said Troughton. 'Now we can find out exactly what they're up to! And look at this. They're implementing something called the GAG program.'

'What's that about?' said Baker. 'Censorship?'

'Looks like it's to do with taking over all the universities in the free world and indoctrinating them with hatred for Western civilisation. That's what GAG stands for - guilt and grievance.'

'What do you mean?'

'Guilt for ever benefitting from Western civilisation and grievance for ever suffering from it.'

'Very succinct.'

'Come and look at this,' said Pertwee. 'I think I've found some of the story proposals for the new episodes.'

Baker and Troughton walked over.

'Let's see what the SJWs have got in mind,' said Baker. 'Read one of them out.'

'*The Dorlek-phobia Menace*,' read Pertwee aloud. 'After the Dorlek wars, a large colony of Dorleks emigrates to England, bringing their xenophobic and supremacist philosophy with them. The Dorlek immigrants are welcomed with garlands of flowers and messages of peace by politicians.'

'Oh dear, that won't end well,' said Troughton, with a chuckle.

'After a series of bombing attacks by Dorlek extremists,'

204

continued Pertwee, 'a group of Dorlek-phobic humans protest about further immigration. But these alt-right English racists are defeated by the Doktor, allowing the Dorleks to live in peace in London and invite more of their numbers to come too.'

'I say,' said Troughton with a frown. 'Fancy the Doktor helping the Dorleks. Things have certainly changed since my day. What's the next episode?'

'Looks like a sequel. It's called *Diversity Heaven is a Place on Earth*,' said Pertwee. 'To celebrate diversity, the High Council of London invites Cyber-people, Ice Warmongers, Santorans, Rootons, and Sue-tekh to join the Dorlek immigrants and all live together. Thanks to the power of diversity, everyone lives in peace and harmony. Meanwhile, the Doktor helps a troubled teen Ice Warmonger come out as gay in the macho culture of his people, and teaches the Ice Warmonger elders to create a safe space for gender-dsyphoric Warmonger kids to accept their sexual identity.'

'Good lord,' said Troughton. 'Is this the type of Utopian paradise the SJWs are trying to create? One where Dorleks and Cyber-people live together?'

'Yes, Doktor, it is.'

The voice came from behind them. The three Doktors turned and saw a pale Englishman on a walkway far above them.

'Who the devil are you, sir? said Pertwee.

'My name is George Tudor. I'm the head of SPEED.'

'That's some silly acronym, is it?'

'It's the Socially Progressive Enlightened Engineering Department.'

'Social engineering, eh,' said Troughton. 'So you're one of the Social Justice Warriors. I suppose this is part of your plan to create a Utopian paradise by putting all the disadvantaged groups into positions of power. Are you sure it will work?'

'It already is working. Look at you - we've forced you to regenerate into a woman.'

'That's not the issue,' said Baker. 'Do you realise I suggested a female Doktor way back in the eighties? Anyway, why are you so interested in controlling my adventures?'

'Don't flatter yourself, Doktor. We don't give a damn about your little TV show. It's just a tiny cog in our social engineering program. *Star Wars*, *Star Trek*, the superhero franchises... they're all just ways to instil progressive values in citizens.'

'Is that so?' said Troughton angrily. 'Well I've got a thing or two to say about that.'

'As have I,' said Pertwee.

'And I,' said Baker.

'Forget it, Doktors. You are under our control now.'

There was a blinding flash and the Doktors found their hands and legs bound by separate strings, so that their bodies dangled like marionettes. In addition, their mouths were taped shut.

'The Doktors have been subjugated,' said George Tudor. 'They are now puppets to do our bidding and they will not speak again unless we permit it.'

A different voice spoke up.

'No, but I will.'

'Who are you?' said George Tudor.

The man was sitting in an armchair at the side of the room. He was a nondescript fellow in ordinary clothes.

'I am Dr Why and here is my disclaimer. The words I speak do not represent the views of anyone associated with this TV program, nor of any group of fans of the show. They are simply the views of one independent fan. I call myself Dr Why and I speak only for myself in querying your control of this program and your wider political agenda.'

'Who are you to question the wisdom of the Social Justice

Warriors?' said George Tudor as he descended the stairs to ground level.

'I'm just some guy.'

'Then speak. Let our dialogue begin.'

VI

Dr Why: What right do you have to use science fiction films and TV shows as vehicles for your progressive agenda?

George Tudor: We have every right. It's all part of DUE process towards Ultimate Justice. DUE meaning Diversity. Unity. Equality.

Dr Why: Sounds very noble. So tell me - you support diversity of different cultural groups, but do you allow diversity of opinions?

George Tudor: As long as they agree with progressive ideals. Citizens with non-progressive opinions will be sent to re-education centres.

Dr Why: What do you really mean by diversity?

George Tudor: It is an ideal in which people of all races, genders, and lifestyle choices are included in public life as equal partners.

Dr Why: Sounds good in principle. Still, I have questions. You proclaim unity as an ideal, but are not your SJW beliefs based on identity politics, a system that divides people up into teams based on those very categories - race, gender, and so on - that you mention?

George Tudor: We divide, then re-unite people in a way that pleases us.

Dr Why: You say you're progressive. Progress towards what? What is your end goal?

George Tudor: Equality. A state of perfect Social Justice in which all races and genders enjoy equal power. We will raise up the poor and dispossessed. We will force all cultural groups to live together in love and harmony.

Dr Why: You speak of love, yet your movement seems to encourage hatred towards one demographic - straight, white males - that has been declared the enemy of all others.

George Tudor: It stands to reason that if other groups are to be lifted up, white males must be removed from positions of power. White males have had too much power for too long. They must be brought down a peg and other types put in their place.

Dr Why: I suppose after the female Doktor, there will be a black Doktor, an LGBT Doktor, and an Islamic Doktor?

George Tudor: We will look to represent all minority groups in an inclusive way that models progressive ideals.

Dr Why: That sounds like a corporate mission statement.

George Tudor: We do indeed have a commitment to excellence in policies that are inclusive of all cultural and lifestyle groups.

Dr Why: Why are you SJWs so obsessed with this racial and gender stuff? It's pathological.

George Tudor: We want justice for the less powerful groups - women, people of colour, gays, immigrants. Their voices have been silenced, their stories marginalised. We will right that social wrong by bringing them all to centre stage.

Dr Why: I understand that all people want to take their place on the stage and tell their stories - but why not start your *own* science fiction TV shows?

George Tudor: Our takeover of this program is a political statement. It's an act of conquest, to transform a quintessentially English TV show starring a male actor. It is a small part of our mission to transform England itself.

Dr Why: What gives you the right to transform England? Who are you people?

George Tudor: We are warriors for love and social equality. We combat hate in all its forms.

Dr Why: By inciting grievance and resentment everywhere you go?

George Tudor: By fighting you, Dr Why, and others like you. You must be a misogynist if you oppose the new female Doktor.

Dr Why: I don't oppose the female Doktor so much as all the rubbish that goes with it - like the way you treat the show as a tool of indoctrination. I mean, you turned Capaldi into a cringing PC cuck in his own regeneration story and used a caricature of Hartnell to lecture the fans about sexism. You're browbeating the old fans, talking down to them.

George Tudor: The fans are ignorant. They must be socially engineered with progressive values in our re-education centres.

Dr Why: You mean brainwashed with identity politics, like students in universities today.

George Tudor: Our 'identity politics,' as you call them, are based on love and inclusiveness.

Dr Why: They seem to be about setting one group against another. It's based on grievance, even when the grievance is irrational.

George Tudor: Such as?

Dr Why: Such as encouraging women to feel personally aggrieved against men for things that happened hundreds of years ago, that have nothing to do with anyone alive today.

George Tudor: Men are guilty and must pay reparations for past sins.

Dr Why: Why? You think men are some kind of gestalt entity and women are another? It's nonsense - but I'm sure there are plenty of opportunists out there who'll lap it up. This is typical identity politics - putting millions of different individuals in big blobby groups like they're all the same, and treating them like one person. The complexities of life get dumbed-down and you encourage everyone to feel permanently hard done by. Except the white males, of course. They're supposed to hate themselves and pay reparations for historical sins they never committed. All this as part of your glorious push for justice by championing your endless parade of victims.

George Tudor: Well, we *are* sick of white males. They are fundamentally evil and must be phased out.

Dr Why: But *you're* a white male.

George Tudor: Yes. I am fundamentally evil and must be phased out.

Dr Why: Why are you so guilty? Who has indoctrinated you into this self-hatred?

George Tudor: I have my orders. It is not for me to question them.

Dr Why: Yes, it is, you fool. Especially something as fundamental as that. No person should accept a belief system that encourages them to hate themselves and their own culture.

George Tudor: It's really for the best that male power is eroded. Europe must be ceded to alternative government so it can be re-made for a progressive future.

Dr Why: You mean globalisation?

George Tudor: Europe must stop being so white. Western civilisation will pay the price for its imperial arrogance.

Dr Why: Is this the reason for your obsession with multiculturalism and diversity? So Europe will cease to be mainly white and Westernised?

George Tudor: Diversity is our strength. Europe must become less European for the sake of progress towards equality.

Dr Why: Why? The Japanese don't try to dilute their cultural identity. Nor do the Africans, sub-continental Indians, or the Islamic nations. Why should Europeans?

George Tudor: Because Europeans are guilty.

Dr Why: Of creating Western civilisation?

George Tudor: Yes - and trying to spread it to other cultures through imperialism.

Dr Why: You focus only on the bad aspects and ignore its value and achievements. Even the empire building wasn't done just for selfish reasons but because they believed in the worth of European civilisation.

George Tudor: Pure arrogance.

Dr Why: There was some arrogance, sure, but better that than the self-destructive folly you encourage. Such as your ridiculous open borders policy.

George Tudor: The borders are open due to our great compassion for the refugees from war torn lands. We act from humanitarian ideals in letting them in.

Dr Why: I agree theirs is a heartrending plight, but what are the long term consequences of your policy? I'd better save this complex topic for a later discussion. But why should I trust you? You're saying now your only motive is compassion, but a minute ago you were talking about European guilt and arrogance. What's your real agenda?

George Tudor: Of course there is guilt. We, the Social Justice Warriors, will punish Europe by forcing mass immigration upon it, so Europe will be transformed from within. This is karma, as decided by the Social Justice Warrior High Council. Germany will be punished for the sin of Nazism by being forced to accept high numbers of immigrants. England will be punished for its past imperialism in the same way.

Dr Why: You do realise all the Nazis are dead, right?

George Tudor: They must pay for their sins.

Dr Why: They already did. Most of them were killed, and those who survived paid their own price with their country in ruins. But no one alive in Germany today had anything to do with what happened in the war years. In the same way, no English person alive had anything to do with the empire building of the past. Still you adopt this absurd gestalt thinking in which you try to impose a collective guilt upon them all.

George Tudor: Your arguments mean nothing. We will impose multiculturalism on Europe and force the citizens to like it. We will brainwash and browbeat them into accepting it, on pain of being called racists if they do not.

Dr Why: So - this is your cowardly weapon of intimidation. To brand anyone a racist who dares question the fundamental transformation of their own nation.

George Tudor: We will do it to you too, Dr Why. We will destroy you, grind you underfoot as you deserve. We will declare you a white supremacist.

Dr Why: That is a lie. I don't believe any race is better or worse than another. That doesn't mean I have to think mass uncontrolled immigration is a good idea - especially of those people whose beliefs are incompatible with the West. I mean, you Social Justice Warriors support gay rights, the empowerment of women, and tolerance of other cultures, don't you?

George Tudor: They are among our core values.

Dr Why: Then suppose there was an English right wing group whose belief system had clear elements of homophobia, misogyny, and xenophobia. You would oppose them, right?

George Tudor: Of course.

Dr Why: So would I. But if there was a non-white group from overseas whose belief system also had clear elements of homophobia, misogyny, and xenophobia, would you oppose them too? Or perhaps import them in large numbers into countries with liberal, democratic values?

George Tudor: If they were non-white immigrants, that would be different. Their presence would add to cultural enrichment and diversity.

Dr Why: And what if I queried the wisdom of importing an ideology which, as I said, seemed to contain those non-progressive values - what would you do then?

George Tudor: We would call you an alt-right racist and charge you with hate speech.

Dr Why: But surely I'd be standing up for the same tolerant values you SJWs believe in? How is that hate speech?

George Tudor: Perception is reality. Speak out against progressive ideals and globalisation, and we will destroy you.

Dr Why: I'm sure you can too, given that you control the media, entertainment, and the education system, all of which you use as tools of mass indoctrination. Still, there is another SJW paradox I cannot unravel. My travels have taught me that what makes different cultures special is their uniqueness. Do you agree we should respect each culture's unique identity and traditions?

George Tudor: Of course. That is another core principle.

Dr Why: Then why do you not respect European culture? I agree some multiculturalism and immigration is good - but not if it supplants the traditional culture. If it does, how is it any better than the British imperialism which you consider to have been so evil?

George Tudor: You're being paranoid. Where's the evidence your precious Europe is being changed in the manner you imply?

Dr Why: Here's a clue. Mohammed is now the most popular boys' name for newborn babies in England. There's the future.

George Tudor: So what? Why should England be majority white or European?

Dr Why: It has been so for a couple of millennia at least. What's the point of diluting England so much that it is no longer England?

George Tudor: This is progress towards globalisation.

Dr Why: Why is it *progress* that England is no longer England? Or Germany no longer Germany? Who gave you the right to fundamentally change the nature of a country?

George Tudor: As I said, this is punishment for European imperialism.

Dr Why: But who gave you the right?

George Tudor: I have my orders. It is not for me to question them. Diversity is our strength.

Dr Why: You talk about respecting cultures, but you respect every culture except your own, which you seem determined to diminish. Let's get back to this TV program, which you use as a small tool in your Social Justice crusade.

See, the Doktor character has two aspects to it. In the fictional realm, he is a shape-shifting alien. There is nothing intrinsically in his nature to prevent him being female, black, gay, or whatever you might imagine.

Yet on a meta-level, as a cultural creation, the Doktor is

an English male. You want to change that and do so under the regime of your hateful identity politics. You view his transformation as a conquest, a tool in your social engineering program. In your hands, it becomes an expression of contempt for his cultural origin.

Yes, in one sense, the Doktor can change his identity. Change is his nature. But I object to you using it as a tool in your transformation of the culture that gave him birth.

George Tudor: We need more diversity. Diversity is our strength.

Dr Why: That's just an Orwellian slogan.

George Tudor: Diversity is our strength.

Dr Why: Keep telling yourself that.

George Tudor: Diversity is our strength. Diversity. Unity. Equality. Now, do you have anything else to say before you are arrested and imprisoned for hate speech?

Dr Why: Two things. First, let me repeat that my query is not about the woman Doktor, as such, but the entire nature of your Social Justice Warrior crusade. After all, what are you SJWs really doing? You, on some unknown authority, and while preaching respect for all cultures, enable fundamental changes to the cultural make up of your own country. Anyone who dares question it, you try to silence and intimidate with the charge of being racist or neo-Nazi. Meanwhile, the social changes you enable are almost irreversible in their effects. So, to repeat, who gave you the right?

Second, a word of warning. You have staged your social rebellion by uniting all your 'oppressed' groups in hatred against white males, the supposed privileged class. But what are you going to do now with all that grievance and resentment you stirred up? Sure, it was useful as fuel in your righteous crusade. But good luck getting all those victim groups to unite in harmony once you've got rid of the demographic that acts as a lightning rod to absorb all the anger you've stirred up. You're dreaming if you think they'll all unite as one harmonious society. They'll simply turn on each other, and some other group will become the main target. So - good luck with your glorious Utopia. You're going to need it.

VII

George Tudor walked back up the stairs to the walkway far above Dr Why. When he reached the top, he stared down from his lofty perch at the man in the armchair.

'It doesn't matter what you say, Dr Why. Your words will be censored and deleted, just as you will be yourself. There is no escape for you, and we will not rest until full Social Justice is achieved and Europe entirely subdued. However I will release your feeble Doktors and let them return to their own time zones. They have no power here.'

George Tudor turned and walked away, flicking a switch as he went. Troughton, Pertwee, and Baker lost their gags and the strings binding them.

'What happened?' said Pertwee. 'My memory seems to have been erased. Who are you, sir?'

The man stood up from his armchair.

'I'm Dr Why. I'm here so you don't have to say anything controversial. I'm just questioning the Social Justice Warriors on behalf of some of your fans.'

'Have you devised a plan to oppose them?' said Troughton.

218

'No,' said Dr Why. 'They're too powerful. They control all our social institutions and the means of indoctrination - at the same time posing as the underdogs fighting for freedom. Not even *you* can go up against such insidious dominion.'

'I'm sure we can think of something,' said Baker.

'No,' said Dr Why. 'This is my time period, so I'm stuck with it. You can get away, though. Leave while you can.'

'You never know,' said Troughton. 'Perhaps the SJWs will succeed in creating their social Utopia.'

'Then they will have proven me wrong, but I doubt any Utopia founded on hate can sustain itself for long.'

'We'll see,' said Pertwee. 'In the meantime - I'm going back to the past.'

'And I'll go to the future,' said Baker. 'See how it turns out.'

'I'm off too,' said Troughton. 'Somehow, this whole mission seems like a waste of time.'

Suddenly there was a flash, and Tennant and Smith appeared out of thin air.

'We've done it, Baker,' said Tennant. 'We successfully reverse-engineered ourselves through ten time dimensions to infiltrate SJW HQ. Hey - how'd you get in here, anyway?'

'Never mind,' said Troughton. 'We're leaving.'

'Gee, thanks for allowing me to participate in this story,' said Smith. 'Very inclusive of you.'

One by one, the Doktors departed until Dr Why was left standing alone. And for the time being, that was all she wrote.

She?

Who has written this?

There was a noise behind him. Dr Why turned around and his eyes widened. Then he smiled, nodded, and walked away.

Author's Note:

If you liked this book, *The Tightarse Tuesday Book Club*, help spread the word. Tell a friend... or five friends. Your support is important, and much appreciated.

Also Available

Books By Duncan Smith

The Vortex Winder
The Maelstrom Ascendant
Cultown
The Vast and the Spurious

Contact

Books and albums can be ordered from www.vortexwinder.com, or on Amazon or Book Depository.
   Alfadex Books can be contacted on matthew.alfadex@gmail.com.

Website - www.vortexwinder.com

The Vortex Winder

When fading rocker, Jimmy Brandt, saves the life of an insect, his own life is forever changed. The insect turns out to be an advanced being who gives him the 'Vortex Winder,' a device which grants a different special power each week. Each power leads to unexpected results.

Jimmy makes a comeback to rock music and records his album. Yet his comeback is a quest within a quest. Driven by the Vortex Winder, Jimmy makes an amazing journey. From a simple job interview, to a love affair in Germany, or a harrowing stint in a foreign prison, the adventures of Jimmy Brandt are always a surprise. Trailed by his mentor, Iolango, and his tormentor, Elijinx, Jimmy follows the events of his life to a stunning conclusion.

The Maelstrom Ascendant

Rocker Jimmy Brandt has given up on his dreams. He's settled down in the suburbs with his girlfriend and cat... until strange forces tempt him back to his former life. Soon he faces a choice between good and evil – and life is so rewarding when you turn to the dark side.

Flying high again, Jimmy battles divas, despots, and most of all, himself. Yet the higher you fly, the further you can fall. Only an old, forgotten friend can save him. But does he want to be saved?

Cultown

Thomas Swan forms the Milinish, a cult with an odd mix of scientific and religious beliefs.

From humble beginnings in Sydney, the Milinish moves overseas to become the fastest growing cult in America. Yet Swan's mad reign spirals out of control. Finally, on the brink of disaster, he decides to tell all.

Here, in the ultimate inside story, Thomas Swan reveals the secrets and scandals inside the Milinish, the greatest cult of the 21st century.

'Exposes not just the cultishness of religion, but of science too. This is the best novel yet written on the trouble between science and religion.'

J. Williams, Fuse.

The Vast and the Spurious - 25 Problems for Feminism

There is a backlash against feminism. Some will dismiss it as misogyny, but this is a mistake. Feminism can no longer assume it owns the high moral ground. Unless it answers its critics it will never gain popular support, and the gender wars will rage 'til doomsday.
Some see feminism as a fight for justice. Others see it as a zealous regime. One thing's for sure - there's more anger between men and women than ever before.

"Whether for the uninitiated, the curious, or the indoctrinated, this book offers a witty rebuttal to modern feminist claims and exaggerations. Grounded in common sense and empathy, it makes the rational case, too rarely heard, for harmony between the sexes and respect for men's contributions."

Janice Fiamengo, Professor of English, University of Ottawa, Canada, and editor of *Sons of Feminism: Men Have Their Say.*